TUNNEL VISION

ALSO BY TANYA EBY

Easy Does It

Blunder Woman

Pepper Wellington And The Case
Of The Missing Sausage

Foodies Rush In

TUNNEL VISION

and Other Stories

From The Edge

TANYA EBY

EBY INK LLC
GRAND RAPIDS, MICHIGAN

Eby Ink LLC
PO Box 68872
Grand Rapids, MI 49516

First Printing: January 2013
ISBN- 978-0-9860133-2-4
Cover design by David Kolenda

Visit the author's website www.TanyaEby.com

For all of you who have read my blog and Facebook posts and have encouraged me to keep going.

Tunnel Vision

"Abandon every hope, ye who enter"

–Dante's Inferno

PROLOGUE

Dark. Cold. Aboveground, a fierce storm of ice and wind caught the world as the gales rushed through the bay. Teacup ships cracked on the shore. The wind—now a rabid beast—howled and moaned as it tore through woods. The storm encased trees in glass, bent their backs, shook them to the roots, lifted saplings as easily as picking a mushroom and spun an outhouse near Kids' Creek. We huddled in our wards, in private rooms, in cells, in the corridors, in the crevices. We moaned, too.

In the Tunnels, all was quiet.

Except for the panting.

Deep in the Tunnels, the storm above was barely a breath. It could not touch the earth's heart, only the surface, and we huddled deep below in the place of no light. We were darkness and shadows blending. The Tunnels surrounded us and hid us.

We crawled from our caged rooms. The iron bars did not hold us in—not as they intended—but kept the outside world from interfering with us, which is exactly what we wanted. The bars were iron, the doors locked, but we were liquid and slipped down into the corridors, melted into the floor, swirled down, down, down to the place where she hid. Blackness, thick as molasses, swaddled us.

You could not see her if you looked; but we could see everything. We were everyone and everywhere. We knew she was there even though she was quiet as a secret, and we tried to swallow our laughter, our excitement. There she was, beyond one of the final bends of The Tunnels, sitting on the cold cement ground, pressed up against the weeping, stone walls. She was a patch of gray cloth and milky skin against the black of the Tunnel walls. We knew what to look for and how to look. We closed our eyes and listened. That's how you find things in the dark. Not with your eyes, but your ears. Listen. Listen. We hissed the word, sent it slithering through the tunnels until the sound found her and bounced back.

Sharp breathing, the panting of a feral animal, she crouched, waiting. She put her finger to her lips. Hussshhhhh, she whispered, as much to herself as to us. We mustn't let the doctors and nurses know. They must never know. Hussshhhhh. It lost the sense of a word and became just another part of the ice storm above. Hussshhhhh: her finger to her lips. Our fingers rose to our lips and answered her. We would hush too. Only the wind and cracking of ice would be our voice.

She was a feral dog and protected her growing secret: a bone in her stomach.

4

But it was not a bone, of course. No single bone grew and changed shape. No. She carried so much more. In the corners of our minds, we knew what happened. She was one person becoming two. She did not associate it with the animal functions she'd done countless of times with men, although some of us knew it had caused the swelling of her stomach. Men. It's always the men who do those things.

We had watched her in the woods, in the doctor's office, and one night down in the Tunnels itself. Who could blame her such pleasure? We were envious. We watched the orderly around her. How he first noticed her. Tried to not notice her. How his hand would lightly touch her back when he asked a question. "Would you like to take your walk now?" he'd say. He never ordered her, never told her, "Take a walk! Put on your shoes! Stop your wailing!" No. To her, he was kind. He offered her the soft-kindness that hid a sharp edge of malice. He wanted. He was a dog. He gave her things, yes—extra bread, a bit of cake, a blue ribbon—but he wanted all the more. He even gave her a pearl button. She kept it under her tongue to keep it a secret as well.

She showed him the dark place. Of course the dark place between her legs, but more than that. Our hidden place. The Tunnels. The Tunnels were built under the asylum to transport refuse, they said, but really it was to hide us. To hide those of us here they did not want the outside world to see. There were extra arms to The Tunnels the doctors had forgotten about over the years. We think the architect may have secretly been one of us, for he'd built us a hidden playground. A place where we could be free.

She showed the orderly the way down. Through twisted doorways and passages, the intricate system of bends and curves in the endless dark. She took his hand, and he blindly followed her until, surrounded by dark, she let him find her with his mouth, and that had been the beginning of the end for him. They met there countless times to grunt and paw at each other, to nuzzle like dogs. He became an animal too, we thought with satisfaction. And aren't all men this close to being like us? Take away the clothes and the jobs and give them something to hunger for, and we are no different. We are all animals, especially when we give over to feeling. He licked and panted and eventually gave her pleasure in a way very different than the button. The button at least she could keep.

Then he was gone. Fired. Let go. Humiliated. Moved on with his wife and children. She did not know. She did not understand. She did not question or care. He became a memory, or perhaps an illusion. She couldn't tell. She understood secrets. She understood Hussshhh. She understood how to be very, very quiet even when under incredible pain. She could be completely quiet. In fact, she never said a word.

We helped her keep silent.

When the child emerged from between her legs, the woman did not cry out or scream. Her daughter entered a world of darkness and silence. We caught Alma, her entrance into the world. We cleaned her mother up, helped her to her bed. We took the child and hid her. When her mother slipped from this world altogether at, we think, the same time the Great Oak in the gardens split in half with the weight of ice, silence overwhelmed the tunnels.

The child understood us, you see. She was happiest in the darkness of our supportive arms.

We vowed we would watch over her, protect her, nurture her. She would be our daughter, a daughter born from our dark minds, raised to live the way we would live if not for the rules. We offered a hundred hands to protect her. A hundred pairs of eyes to watch over her. We wanted nothing in return.

We thought we knew everything, sensed everything. Somehow, though, we didn't see what was coming. How could we? We understand this thing they call madness, our own and each other's. We have learned to navigate those waters. It's easy to do. Just figure out the way each mind bends and go with it; do not try to reshape the path. We thought we were in control.

At first, we did not recognize Dr. Kinney as one of us. No. Only afterwards, after pawing through his diaries, comparing notes, and sending information through the wards, person to person, did we fully understand what had happened, and our understanding comforted us. We did not recognize his madness because he was not like us. No. Dr. Kinney was not mad; he was evil. There is a profound difference.

Pure silence filled the Tunnels at the birth of our beloved Alma. There would be silence for years to come. Only aboveground did the world cry out and moan.

PART ONE – Asylum

Northern Michigan Insane Asylum features sprawling green hills and landscaping as relaxing as it is beautiful. Your loved one will be as well tended as our gardens. The asylum follows the Kirkbride Plan in which patients are treated with kindness, comfort and pleasure. Indeed, restraints are considered barbaric. A chaotic mind must have peace and beauty in which to flourish, and a place of safety to do work. Patients at the Northern Michigan Insane Asylum will be comforted by music, gardening, and the great gentle beauty of Nature herself.

–Promotional Material for The Northern Michigan Insane Asylum, 1915

The Board of Directors at the Northern Michigan Insane Asylum request additional funding to support not only its current residents, but also to expand the program. While we follow the Kirkbride Plan of treating all patients with kindness, comfort and pleasure, there are certain minds that are so badly fractured they need additional care. The Northern Michigan Insane Asylum features a system of tunnels connecting the more than 4 acres of facilities. This allows for the transfer of unsightly goods such as refuse, as well as maintenance issues to the facility. Additionally, there is ample space located in the basement of the facility for those members of our society who are too disturbed to participate in the outside world. They receive kindness, understanding and the best scientific practices possible. Please consider our request for additional support . . .

−Grant request for funding to the State of Michigan, 1920

ONE

Northern Michigan Insane Asylum

"Course it's raining now so you can't tell, but this place is something special," Bill Pepperidge said, nodding to the windshield as the wiper skidded across it.

Little good the wiper did in the rain, Dr. Elliott Kinney thought. He hoped the old groundskeeper knew the way to the asylum without benefit of being able to actually see the road through the downpour.

Kinney clutched his leather bag to his chest as if to shield him from the cold. It held his most important research on personality disorders and possible treatments; it was, in essence, his entire life's purpose within a satchel of leather.

The rain fell in heavy sheets, pounding the tin roof of the truck around them and bowing maple trees forward. *This is what it's like to be stuck in a locomotive about to careen off a bridge,* Kinney thought. He breathed. Tried to clear his mind. He must stay focused and not slip into fantasies, as he was sometimes prone to do.

Dr. Kinney tried to get a sense of the grounds and the much-heralded flower and vegetable gardens, but everything was rain and dark and shadows. The truck twisted and turned on the road, and he silently assured himself they would not careen off a bridge (they were on a simple dirt road after all) and, above all, he would not let his stomach react. The last thing he needed was to enter his new place of employment with sick on his shirt. He silently damned his weak stomach, but controlled its churning by clutching his bag tighter to his chest.

The truck lurched and heaved.

"Sorry about that, Doctor," Pepperidge said after splashing through a large pothole.

Kinney tried to calm his mind. The sound of the wipers skidding across the windshield was almost melodic. He could focus on that. Better to focus on that than the condition of the heap they traveled in. Kinney regretted allowing the groundskeeper to pick him up at the hotel. He should have brought his car and travelled here in the safe, bright calm of morning.

Kinney moved his foot, stunned to see a flash of brown beneath it. It was the dirt road, spinning under them, as seen through a hole in the floor. If he didn't fall through one of the rust holes in the floor, surely the bumping of the Model-A pickup would rattle his brain, perhaps so much he would have to be admitted as a patient instead of its newest doctor. The wipers thumped. The rain hit hard against them. *A locomotive chugging towards my death.*

Pepperidge continued, "I know you can't see it now so you'll have to take my word for it, but when the sun is shining and it's coming through those maples, you'd swear the trees were on fire or something. In a good way, of course. Like a beautiful kind of . . . " He paused and tugged on the brim of his hat. "Magic," he said with a firm nod, as if he'd decided that was just the word. "Shame that Great Oak didn't last. Most beautiful tree I've ever seen. Lost that in an ice storm near twenty years ago. Cracked clean down the center as if split with God's hatchet."

He wrenched the steering wheel, made a sharp turn, the muscles in his thin arms flexing. Kinney guessed him to be in his mid-sixties, but he still had the muscles of a young man. He had more muscles than Kinney.

The truck shifted and bounced, and Dr. Kinney leaned against the window, certain he was going to fall out. If he had been a praying man, he would have whispered a prayer of protection. He did not whisper.

"Beauty is important here, you know," the groundskeeper continued.

Dr. Kinney nodded, though he doubted the old man could see him. He was not surprised when the old man continued talking.

"Course you probably know of Kirkbride's ideas that insane people need beauty and music and all that sort. You

14

wouldn't believe how much time I spend pruning bushes and planting bulbs. Some of the less crazy ones I have help me, but you wouldn't want to give just any of them a shovel, let alone a hoe. Not complaining, of course. Glad to have a job, especially with things they way they are. Beauty though, I don't know. I don't see much point to it, unless you're walking a woman home or something. You one of them kind of doctors? You believe that beauty is important to these people? You believe they can be healed?"

"It's not a matter of belief," Kinney said.

"Exactly!" Pepperidge said as if this was the answer he had been looking for. "I say toss 'em in the place and lock the doors. Keep that ugliness inside and away from others. Course, they let them walk the grounds and pick flowers and such, and I guess they do all right. At least, they're tucked away on this property. And I think the flowers and trees are mostly for show. It's not about beauty curing these twisted people. Nope. It's about covering them up. You'll see, doctor. There's all sorts of ugliness here. They don't even let the real crazies walk around. The real crazy ones are kept elsewheres."

Kinney did not respond. He had three years of experience with the mentally deranged–a lifetime of experience if you included his dealings with his family. He would still be working in Detroit if the incident there could have been smoothed over. Kinney firmly believed science required aggressive, progressive thinking, and, at times, action.

Bill Pepperidge slammed the truck into park, shaking the thoughts from Kinney's mind.

"We're here," Pepperidge said with a grin, exposing teeth like a row of yellow corn. "Building Fifty." He nodded at the expansive building that seemed to have been born from the rain and shadows and would surely fade when morning came. "Hope you're ready for this."

Kinney looked up. How could he not have noticed this building before? It was massive. The dark and the rain seemed to have sucked the building into its embrace, encasing it in shadows, but now, parked in front of its imposing doors, the size of the place awed Kinney. The white brick seemed to reach up to heaven itself, almost as if grasping. The building extended beyond his periphery vision, making him feel surrounded. In actuality, he *was* surrounded.

The Northern Michigan Insane Asylum was a sprawling campus featuring dozens of large buildings with three large kitchens and separate wards, segregating the sexes. Cottages and farms sprinkled the grounds.

Dr. Elliott Kinney gathered his courage, nodded once, opened the truck door and braced himself for the onslaught. There was a hint of ice in the drops and the fierce rain and cold cut at his skin and made him briefly feel still alive. With his beloved bag poised over his head to protect him from the rain, he ran to the doors. The groundskeeper called him, but the rain obscured the words.

TWO

Kinney stood before two great wooden doors shaded him from the thrashing rain, but not the icy fingers of the wind. The rain found him, as it seemed to be shooting sideways.

"You'll be fine inside!" Pepperidge bellowed. "What better place for protection from a storm than an asylum?" The groundskeeper might have barked a laugh, but the wind and rain and the solid screech of the doors opening drowned it out.

Kinney walked in, illumined by the truck's headlights until Pepperidge quickly reversed, leaving Kinney to an impenetrable darkness. He waited for his eyes to adjust to the dull electric lights.

He wasn't sure what he'd anticipated upon his arrival–perhaps to enter the great facility alone and in solitude. He

17

would call out for assistance *Hello, anyone here?*, and listen to his words echo along the corridors, then find his way to his room alone. At after nine in the evening on a Tuesday, amidst a swirling storm, he did not expect what happened next: Two rows of nurses and orderlies, stood stiff as starched shirts before him. The men wore white pants and collared white shirts; the women in white dresses with white aprons.

He did not expect to walk through the aisle they made for him and certainly had not anticipated the applause. Two men stood at the end of the line, one dressed in a dark suit, the other in dark working clothes. He guessed the gentleman would be one of the board members who had hired him to assist Doctor Christopher Grooms, and Kinney was not disappointed. This, at least, fit with his expectations, as did the appearance of the place. It looked just like the publicity photos, though, perhaps, slightly more shadowed and mildewed.

The front room was expansive with high ceilings. The floor was slick marble and polished to a sheen. One would think, entering this room, they had arrived at a Lord and Lady's mansion; not a facility for the criminally and terminally insane. Kinney appreciated the architecture of the place and the reasoning behind it. If you must hold people with diseased spirits, then hold them in a place of supreme order and cleanliness to help disguise the inherent nature of the place.

Kinney noted the neat line of orderlies and nurses, their uniforms and body language crisp, their faces staring not at him but seemingly into nothingness. He removed his hat and smoothed his hair. Someone coughed. Kinney adjusted his tie, clutched his bag firmly and began his descent into the belly of the room. Dripping wet, he nodded to the nurses and orderlies and walked down the aisle, his shoes clicking on the floor. There was no sound save for his feet and the rainwater falling from his coat. Even though he was wet and certainly bedraggled looking, he knew if he held his head high and walked with purpose, he would immediately communicate his role here. He was a doctor and was to be respected.

The staff averted their eyes as he passed, and for a moment, Kinney felt almost like a bride walking down an aisle to hushed anticipation.

A thin gentleman with spectacles waited at the bottom of a winding staircase. "Hear, hear!" he called warmly, and the staff responded with polite applause. "Welcome, Dr. Kinney!" He reached out to grab Kinney's hand, and the applause quieted as quickly as it had started. "Doctor Kinney, a pleasure! A pleasure! Do come in." His handshake was warm, firm, and sustained. "I am Mr. Harrison, Edward Harrison, and this is Mr. Briggart." Mr. Harrison dropped his hand and it was promptly captured in the meaty embrace of Mr. Briggart.

Mr. Briggart wore a flannel shirt, suspenders and trousers. He was so big, the fabric nearly screamed with the effort to contain him.

19

"Name's Harvey," Mr. Briggart said, his voice deep and vibrating in his chest. His palm was cool and moist. When he ended the handshake, Kinney discreetly wiped his palm against the fabric of his coat. "I'm in charge of the facility management," Briggart finished.

"And I'm the President of the Board," added Mr. Harrison. "I do apologize that the rest of the Board is not here to meet you, but that will change in due time. In due time." Mr. Harrison took in Kinney's appearance. "Ah," he said, "Come along now. I'll have someone carry your bags to your room." He motioned, and the precise white lines of nurses and orderlies dispersed, as silently as snow falling.

Briggart bent to take Kinney's bag from him, but Kinney shook his head.

"Not this one," he said, his voice soft but firm. "You can take all the others."

Briggart looked at Kinney for a moment too long then gave a discreet nod of his buffalo-size head.

Mr. Harrison adjusted his spectacles and issued a small grunt. He continued: "We have you stationed in Building Fifty for the time being, then we will move you to one of the cottages on our site. Of course, should you choose, you may want to purchase a home near the waters. Traverse City is beautiful. That is, of course, if you stay." He looked at Kinney as if expecting a response.

"Of course," Kinney said. He had not made up his mind about his future at this establishment. He cared little for a cozy home. He was here to work. His patients would decide for him. If he was able to accomplish his research here, then he could happily stay here indefinitely. He adjusted the grip on his bag.

"Very good then, very good." Mr. Harrison grunted again. "To your room and then we shall have dinner and a tour, if that is all right with you."

Kinney hesitated to pull out his pocket watch. The weight of traveling from Detroit played heavily on him. The last thing he wanted right now was a tour. He wanted to curl up and sleep. He had not slept in so very long, and the rain sang to him like a heavy lullaby.

"Ah," Mr. Harrison said, as if reading Kinney's thoughts. Mr. Harrison adjusted his spectacles then winked. "Of course, perhaps you prefer a little solitude tonight. I will show you to your room, and we can reconvene in the morning for breakfast. At that point, I can turn you over to Dr. Grooms and the support team. Will that be to your liking?"

Kinney offered a smile thinned by fatigue, but heavy with gratitude.

"To your room then!"

Kinney followed Edward Harrison up the ornate staircase and down three or more corridors. The hallways replicated each other: long white floors and dark wooden doors to marked and unmarked rooms.

"You'll learn all this in time," Mr. Harrison said over his shoulder as he quickly navigated the labyrinth. They walked on and on, and Kinney struggled to keep up. "Ah.

And here we are." Mr. Harrison stopped in front of a door labeled DR. E. KINNEY, withdrew a skeleton key and opened the door.

The room was expansive, with an ornate bed. Kinney's bags already waited for him, dripping slightly with rain. A basket with bread and cheese also greeted him.

"How on earth . . . " Kinney started.

"Magic," Mr. Harrison said soberly. "In other words, Harvey Briggart. He's a master at coming and going, as is most of the support staff. They move around like whispers. All so that we do not disturb the graceful minds of our patients. It's really quite astounding. And on that note, I will leave you to your solitude." He adjusted his spectacles, grunted once more, turned and was gone.

Doctor Elliott Kinney entered his room and was alone. He had been alone for two years now, and though he appreciated the quiet, he found no comfort in his solitude— not when the presence of his sister Rose was almost so palpable he could smell the cloying hint of her perfume lingering in the air.

Kinney sat on the bed in the Spartan room. The room easily could have been for a well-off patient instead of for a doctor. One mirror clung to the white walls, and there were no pictures or artwork. He saw the dim ghost of frames removed and nails abandoned by the previous tenant. The dresser was made of dark wood. A patchwork quilt, thin and faded from years of use, covered the bed. The fabric seemed to be made of old dresses, perhaps the outfits women inmates wore; inmates who never left.

He tried not to breathe too deeply. He methodically opened and unpacked his two bags of clothing, placed his ironed shirts and pants on hangers, and his undergarments and socks in separate drawers. Kinney lined up his toiletries in the order they belonged on his vanity.

Once he'd put away his belongings, he changed out of his wet clothes and into a dry cotton shirt and boxers. He smoothed the covers on his bed and sat. He listened to the rain fall. He took a deep breath. Finally, at last, he was here.

"Elliott?"

He turned his head toward the sound. He'd thought he'd heard his name in a voice as familiar as his own. A female voice–soft as a secret. Of course, it was just the wind or fatigue starting to crack the boundaries in his mind between sleep and alertness. He needed to rest. He had needed to rest for two years. Perhaps now he was here and could finally return to his important research, he could find the peace that had been absent from his life. He was counting on it.

That peace would not come on this night, though. When sleep finally took him, it did not soothe him. Even though this was a new place, a new start, it seemed his sister had followed him again, even into the deepest of shadows; and she was with him still.

THREE

That first night we sent spies to watch over him. Who was this stranger? What would his presence mean for us? Could he heal us? Was it possible? Did we even want it? We would wait and see. We would watch and monitor and decide.

We tried to warn Alma, but she was drawn to him the way a meteor is drawn to earth. "Do not go near him," we pled, because we knew the ways of men. Some of us are men, and we know . . . we know . . . we know.

"I won't. I promise," she said, and we believed her. It was the first time she'd lied to us. Already he was changing her. The way dirt will muddy a perfect stream of water.

FOUR

Kinney dreamed of walking through a cherry orchard when in bloom. White blossoms laced with pink clung to the trees. Miles and miles of green hills and cloudlike blossoms surrounded him. The lake stretched out in front of him like a blue strip across the horizon.

He could feel her reaching to him, and he went to her, slowly, as if she would disappear like smoke if he approached too quickly. She did not. He wrapped his arms around her, pulled her close to his chest. He could feel her. He could honestly feel her.

He unfastened the top two buttons of her dress, at the nape of her neck, tilted her head forward and lifted her dark hair so that her spine rose before him. Then, slowly, he lowered his lips, and he kissed the skin that lay exposed and vulnerable before him. Wanting filled him, a desperate wanting that washed over him like a wave, followed by another surge of shame so deep it turned his spirit to ice.

"Love me again, Elliott." She spoke the words they vowed never to say aloud.

It was his rage that answered her and he said, "No."

He tugged tightly on her hair, wrenched her neck backwards, and tilted her lips up to him. She seemed to stop breathing. She wanted this, he knew. Worse still, he wanted it, too. He pushed her away.

"Never," he whispered, his voice an angry hush, "Never speak of this again. What happened never happened, do you understand me? Do you?"

She looked at him and smiled.

*

"Good morning, sir, I do apologize for waking you and coming into your chambers and all, sir."

Kinney opened is eyes to see a young girl looking plaintively at him. Her voice had an Irish musicality to it, and her coloring spoke of relatives from distant shores. Her freckled face flushed, and red curls threatened to burst free of the white bonnet. Kinney realized he was not dreaming. No. This was real, as was the young girl nineteen or so, and her hand rested against his shoulder, touching the fabric of his shirt, burning with heat to his very skin.

"I'm Mallie Lyn Peters, sir. I help with cleaning and such, sir." She covered her mouth with her hands. "For the doctors, sir, not for the others. There's nurses and specialists who tend to them and I ain't . . ."

Kinney lifted himself in bed, temporarily interrupting the girl. Her face blushed crimson. "Continue," he said.

"I shouldn't of woke you up sir, but Doctor Grooms is here, and he's ready to get you started, and he said I mustn't hesitate but to wake you up directly, and I did too, only first I stopped in the kitchen to grab you a bit of bread, and then I got to talking to one of the attendants, and then well, I ate that piece of bread sir what with Charlie . . . I mean Mr. Young talking on and on and so, and then I remembered that I needed to . . ."

Kinney yawned, none too discreetly. "Thank you, Mallie. If you could . . ."

"You want something to eat? I could go back to the kitchen."

"I'd like to get dressed," he said pointedly. The pink flush to her skin soon deepened to a positive burn.

"Course sir, excuse me sir. I'll wait outside and then show you the way. It's awful easy to get lost in here. Why I've heard about a woman once who . . ."

"Thank you, Mallie. That will be all."

Mallie swallowed hard, curtsied, and then retreated from his room. He waited until the door clicked shut before he removed the quilt.

Kinney gingerly stepped out of his bed, as if expecting pain when he walked, the way a mermaid new to legs would expect and anticipate the prick of a thousand knives with each step of tender feet. The pain did not come, only the sharp rush of cold tile to bare feet. He made a mental note for slippers.

He walked to the window and drew open the curtains. For the first time, he could see the grounds of the Northern Michigan Insane Asylum before him. It was beautiful. Simply beautiful.

The grounds rolled, like great green waves, the color deepened by last night's storm. The trees were all colors of fire: crimson, orange, bright yellow, and bits of pine green. The lawn in front of Building Fifty was ornately landscaped. He could see the perennials had already been trimmed and waited for winter. He imagined the garden would bloom with all the colors of a newborn star in the spring. It was so delicately beautiful, so tenderly balanced Kinney could not believe that brute of a groundsman, Bill Pepperidge, had anything to do with it. This magic garden was surely the work of a wood nymph. Bill Pepperidge could not be responsible for the entire appearance of the massive grounds. Kinney knew someone must orchestrate an army of groundskeepers . . . all of which, he imagined, were inmates who could handle lowbrow work. It was all incorporated and described in the Kirkbride plan to: "provide structured work to focus and sharpen diseased minds".

It was also free labor. Kinney wondered how much money the hospital pulled in from selling the flowers the inmates tended, or milk from the dairy farm they tended, or the vegetables they grew. The Asylum was almost a machine of humming productivity, and no one would be the wiser that such distorted minds had tended to such beauty.

He closed the curtains, firmly shutting out the light and color. It was time to dress and time to begin the walk on his life's new path. As he slipped on his trousers, he wondered, briefly, what price was paid to keep up such beauty, and who exactly paid for it. In Doctor Kinney's experience, beauty was never without its opposite for long.

FIVE

"This way, sir," Mallie said once Kinney emerged from his room, his hair slicked back and still wet from the morning ablutions. She motioned to him and began a brisk pace, her skirts swishing. He watched her worn black shoes escape ahead of him. She walked swiftly, her heels clicking on the polished floors. Again, the hallways spun in a blur of white around him. He was aware of the sound of their shoes echoing on the floors, but also a sort of electric hum—the natural sounds of the asylum stirring to life.

Building 50 was reserved for staff offices, the headquarters, the kitchen, and one of three dining areas. From the literature he'd read, he knew that the men and women's wards branched off from Building 50. He could not, as of yet, hear the patients stirring, but he could feel their presence all around him, as if enwrapped by a giant python just beginning to stir.

Mallie turned a corner and seemed to disappear. Kinney tripped, caught himself from falling and called out "Stop!" Then leaned his head against the cool wall to catch his breath. He heard his blood pumping.

"Oh, dear. I'm so sorry!" she cried. "I forget sometimes that I move too fast. My ma says I'm like a hummingbird. I ought to slow down. And look at you, Dr. Kinney, coughing away like that. You must've caught a cold from coming here in that storm last night."

Kinney held up his hand as much to tell her that he was fine as to get the girl to stop talking. He just needed to catch his breath. Lately it was as if he was asthmatic. His anxiety, something he could control, caused the racing of his heart and shortness of breath.

"We're almost there, sir. I promise."

He nodded, and she led him through a vast network of winding corridors until he arrived, breathless, into a great open room with thirty-foot tall ceilings and twenty or so rectangular, wooden tables, the brown wood stark against the bright white of the walls, floor and ceiling.

"We're in one of the dining rooms, sir," Mallie said. "This one is the largest, but there are . . ."

"Two more. Yes, I've done my homework."

Kinney looked around. Each sturdy table was set for four or more. Tall, thin windows reached from floor to ceiling. Sun didn't so much as pour through the windows but illuminated the space from within. The floor was tiled and scrubbed clean. The effect was of an efficient hospital-like cafeteria, but it still managed to be somewhat homey. Sound seemed to bounce around them, as if they were in a deep cave.

"Is there anything else I can get for you, Dr. Kinney? You know, while you wait for Doctor Grooms." Mallie asked, her Irish accent lilting. "If you wouldn't mind I'd like to be on my way and back to my other duties before Doctor Grooms gets here. He doesn't like to deal so much with the lesser support staff, and I'd just as well like to get about my day, if you don't mind."

He studied her face for a moment. He'd begun his career as a medical doctor but had switched to psychiatry when his sister fell ill. He had trained himself to be sensitive to what the body said as well as how a person spoke. So much meaning clung not to what was said but to how it was voiced and sometimes, more importantly, the words held back.

Mallie's cheeks flushed, which might have been a natural state for her. Something in the tautness of her smile and her eyes did not shine with humor but were dulled from a lack of it. This girl was, for whatever reason, afraid.

"Certainly, Mallie. You are excused."

She curtsied. "Thank you, sir, kindly. If you need anything else, sir, do not hesitate to call for me. You may not always see me about, but I am sir, or someone is who knows where to find me. You have only to call my name."

With a swishing of her skirts, she left.

Kinney walked to the window, the curtains tied back to allow for the sunlight. Funny, one would never guess this was the home of the mentally deranged. Looking at the couples strolling arm in arm, one would think this a place of respite or a grand park, if not for the fact that many of the people wore striped pajamas, their partners clothed in the sterile white of the nurses and orderlies. The couples, all of the same gender, strolled arm in arm. The Northern Michigan Insane Asylum did not mix the sexes.

Separate housing complexes housed the men from the women. Except for the communal walking areas, the place was effectively segregated.

He wondered if the *criminally* insane were as effectively segregated. There must be some place where they resided. It was for their care the he had been summoned, not for the care of simple depressives and drug addicts. No. Dr. Kinney specialized in the psychoses of a higher, or perhaps lower, sort. He'd dedicated his life and scientific methods into curing them by any means possible.

Heavy footsteps preceded a deep, melodic voice.

"Good morning to you, Doctor Kinney. Welcome to your new life."

The man, surely Dr. Grooms, had the sharp chin and bearing of someone used to being obeyed. He was taller than Kinney, and solidly built. Old acne scars flecked his rough skin, and he possessed eyebrows so bushy they appeared almost feral. Dr. Grooms spread his arms open wide and smiled, a smile which did not reach his eyes.

SIX

In life, as things happen, they happen in a linear fashion. One thing follows the next. One foot goes in front of the other and then is followed again. And so the tour of the facilities and grounds did occur in a linear way. Kinney followed Dr. Grooms and listened to him and nodded, and noticed the fierce sunlight and the way their shoes echoed on the spotless floors.

After touring several identical buildings, they worked their way to the small onsite farm—a dairy where patients milked cows and sold the resulting dairy products. Dr. Grooms talked while they walked at a brisk pace, his voice sounding as if he'd stuffed his cheeks with cotton.

"You've been brought on to fill an important vacancy in our staff. It's your research I was most taken with. The idea that a patient can be healed by manipulating or actually taking out a part of the brain." He turned to Kinney and smiled again, while motioning him to hurry along. The palpable scent of cow manure caused Kinney to bring his handkerchief to his nose; the scent had no affect on Grooms.

"There's a doctor in Switzerland who is further along in his research than I am," Kinney admitted.

"Of course, of course. Watch your step, here." Grooms motioned to a pile of manure on the ground. Kinney's stomach roiled. "We are a small facility, doctor. We don't actually expect you to invent anything. We just need to have you actively researching and proving to our financial supporters that we are an institution that thinks forward. For fifty years this establishment has operated under the notion that peaceful work heals the chaotic mind . . . minds like this woman. Stand up, Gerty."

A young woman stood next to the cow she had been milking. She had the widely spaced eyes of an imbecile, harmless and peaceful as the cow. Doctor Grooms coughed and brought a handkerchief to his nose. "You and I both know, Dr. Kinney, that there are people who are much more violent than this girl here. People who don't even understand, let alone recognize, peace and beauty."

"And where do the others work?" Kinney asked.

Dr. Grooms laughed, a chuckle that echoed from the pit of his stomach. "Work? Surely you know better than that. A lucky few, the most disturbed of the bunch, have been set aside. For you, Kinney."

Kinney nodded.

"We'll tour the wards now," Dr. Grooms said. "You'll get your exercise today for sure. Sounds like you could use it from the way you're breathing."

"I am more of an intellectual than an outdoorsman," Kinney admitted.

"All the better."

They exited the small farm and took the long, dirt path back to the center of the campus. The cool air hinted of winter coming. Brown leaves that had been clinging to branches, released their hold and fluttered in the breeze. Kinney pulled his jacket closer and tried to deeply breathe the fresh air, hoping to eradicate the scent of animal.

At last, they reached the buildings that housed the inmates. The main asylum was designed as a long rectangle with two arms branching off it. The distance separated the two sexes, although each side of the ward was nearly identical. Dr. Grooms captained a tidy ship.

As soon as they entered the facility, the smell of sickness covered with medicine replaced the scent of winter. Each ward had separate levels. Inmates with families able to pay for their keep were treated to a wide room with plenty of light and space. Beds had homemade blankets, and fresh flowers brightened the rooms. Music played during parts of the day, and the staff served afternoon tea. After treatments, the patients could retreat to a private room until they felt well enough to return to the shared ward.

The second ward was for inmates who had some income, enough to cover bare expenses. There was no tea, more beds, and the ward had the sterile feel of a hospital.

The final level housed "wards of the state", inmates who could not be trusted out in the open and had no family or money. The conditions of their room was as expected.

As Kinney walked through the rooms, he nodded to inmates. The men and women looked nearly the same, sexless save for the shape of the women's breasts dangling just under the thin fabric of their smocks. He could tell by looking at their faces what conditions they suffered: dementia, schizophrenia, and madness through sexual activity that had caused their brains to rot in their skulls. Some were clearly physically and mentally retarded, some possessed by seizures. It was a range of sorrow and sickness, and the beauty the Kirkbride Plan professed was as flimsy as a sheer curtain hiding the fetid whiff of something rotten.

Kinney wanted to see more. Ached for it. For once, he felt he was here for a purpose. Their blank faces—visages twisted by psychological trauma, bodies twisted by the sheer weight of suffering—Kinney recognized something of himself and was drawn to it.

He toured the men's and women's wings, the dining hall, and the medical ward. But the tour ended there.

"Are we not going to see the other patients? The ones I've been brought here specifically to help?"

Dr. Grooms coughed. "In due time," was all he said.

Dr. Grooms brought Kinney to an office where he was given a coat to wear and forms to fill out.

Everything was precise and orderly.

SEVEN

Everything was precise and orderly even at dinner. The Board of Trustees and their wives gathered to welcome Kinney. He sat at the long table in Building Fifty, the great room transformed into an earl's estate with crisp white linens, a table set for twenty, crystal glasses, china, and polished silver. White rose centerpieces filled the room with the scent of summer and Kinney wondered how it was possible to come by that flower in the late fall. He had been told the occasion was formal, and the Trustees were clad in tuxes and their wives in various shades of silk, the fabric flowing over their bodies like water. Some of the wives made him wish they wore cotton to cover up the folds of their skin a bit more thoroughly, but the fashion suited a few of the younger ones.

Later, Kinney remembered the dinner not in a linear and precisely orderly way, but as an impression. He remembered murmured small talk, the clinking of glasses, the sudden awareness that the gentlemen serving them were patients, disguised in tuxes once owned by the Trustees. The dinner appeared beautiful and wholesome, but still, Kinney saw chips on the china and undercooked meat.

He would reflect later that it was as if the day and all the moments in between had melded together and formed some kind of painting in his mind. There were the cows the patients milked, and the rows of beds the inmates slept in, and the sunlight. The unforgiving sunlight and the shadows. And the eyes. And the pale skin and taut faces looking at him, hiding from him. There was the laughter and the screams in the distance, although he only saw patients who walked and smiled happily.

"And did you enjoy the tour?" The matronly woman sitting next to him asked. She was Dr. Grooms' wife. Their years together made them resemble each other. She was also solidly built, with a strong jaw, and slightly wild eyebrows.

"I did indeed," he said. "Although there is still much of the facility that I'd like to see."

"Have you seen the Tunnels yet?" A gaunt gentleman called from the end of the table. He was on his third glass of wine and well lubricated. A collective murmur went around the table at the mention of the Tunnels.

Kinney immediately became aware of the footman tending to them. He felt his hot breath on the back of his neck and turned, only to find the man standing stiff as a statue and ten paces away.

"What are the Tunnels?" Kinney asked.

"No need to tour that area, Dr. Kinney," Dr. Grooms had said with a hint of ice in his voice. "That is for the *unseemly* things, as we like to say. The transportation of refuse and occasionally of those patients who finally surrender their lives to an illness we cannot cure."

"Don't let Edward scare you," Mrs. Grooms said. "The Tunnels are infamous. Why, some say they're even haunted!"

"Rumors. Silly stories," Grooms said.

"Oh, do tell him about the ghost, Dr. Grooms!" said the gaunt man.

Kinney caught snippets of words from the guests at the table: "I've seen her myself", "rape I heard", "nothing but fallacy", etc.

"Do not fill his head with nonsense. It's only a tale that the locals spin around their dinner tables. Surely a rumor started to scare little children from coming onto our grounds. For that, it is useful." The guests looked at Dr. Grooms expectantly. He gave in. "Margaret, why don't you tell our good Dr. Kinney the tale, then we can be done with it?"

Margaret started speaking almost before her husband had finished. "There's a ghost that roams the halls here! It's a woman, of course, and she's clad only in white."

"She's not clad in white. She's naked. Completely naked!" offered another gentleman, who had an accent that hinted at French roots.

"That, Philippe, is not the story. That is your fantasy!" replied Margaret. The table erupted in laughter.

A younger wife, the type that sort of faded into the wallpaper if you weren't careful, said softly, "I heard there was a woman who gave birth in the tunnels, and she and the child died and . . ." she paused as she realized she spoke out loud and the attention of the room had focused on her. "I'm sorry." Her voice drifted like a feather.

"No, please, madam. Continue," offered Kinney. "The Tunnels?"

"The Tunnels are a vast network built beneath the facility," Dr. Grooms said evenly. "The Tunnels are for refuse and transporting other unseemly matter."

"Like the dead," said the gaunt man, now on a new glass of wine. "And the really insane ones. And the ghosts, of course!"

The younger wife spoke hesitantly again. Soft brown hair, fine as cornsilk, covered her arms. "The mother is searching for her child. You can hear her. During storms."

"No, no, no." said Margaret. "She doesn't want her child. She wants to find a doctor. To help her with a certain *itch*." Again the table laughed, save for Dr. Grooms who said "Margaret" in a tone that set a cold knife to Dr. Kinney's throat. The room chilled.

Dr. Grooms said in a tone to end the subject: "There is a system underneath the campus that you will see in good time, but today, today let us focus on all the pleasantries our facility offers. There are no ghosts, and the rumors about a woman caught in the Tunnels is pure childish fancy."

The table fell into an awkward silence of utensils scraping against the china. Kinney noticed the footmen regarded each other for a moment, as if worried about being questioned. How much of the story was true? Was there a woman who died in the Tunnels? How vast was the system? Were the patients he waited to treat kept down there as well, like shameful secrets?

Kinney chewed his beef and thought how once he'd hid something—something that had been beautiful and had become so unseemly. He could wait to explore the Tunnels and find out what the asylum—and its Board—hid. He would find the madness he'd been brought to address, and he would complete his work. He would find that madness and, like a stubborn root, he would dig it out.

Kinney thought he heard . . . not a moan, exactly, but a kind of whimpering. The wind?

He chewed his meat.

*

We saw Kinney arrive. We wiped raindrops from our shoulders, rung it out of our hair. We slipped into the shadows and watched him stomp down corridors. We noticed his left foot dragged slightly indicating a lift in his shoe. We saw the locked set of his jaw, his skin rough and pitted. We knew those lines; we could almost trace them with out fingers. Those lines were caused by an inner anger—a serpent of rage. We saw him coming and we knew real fear.

He was not sent to help us. No. He was sent to take our spirits away.

We feared for the girl too. For Mallie Lynn Peters who brought us bits of bread and ribbons . . . but mostly we feared for our Alma. We drew her closer to us . . . passed her from shadow to shadow. She spun through the tunnels but we could not keep her there.

How do you keep laughter from rising to the surface? You do not. Even we know that. And so we let her go. We hoped she would be quiet and wait and watch from a distance. Wait and watch until we knew for sure.

Although in retrospect, we knew for sure right away, as soon as Kinney's foot stepped onto the floor of Building Fifty. He had been sent to destroy us, yes. But we would not go down without him. If you drown someone while swimming with them, you must be very careful or they will pull you down with them. We were counting on that. We prepared for a fight.

PART TWO – The Tunnels

The Northern Michigan Insane Asylum features a great expanse of tunnels connecting the separate wards, Building 50, and many of the doctors' residences. This allows for the seamless transportation of goods necessary to the running of the facility, ensuring that your family member will not be aggravated by anything unsightly. Additionally, the Northern Michigan Insane Asylum has separate wards for men, women, and those from higher paying members of our society. There are separate wards for those patients of lower classes who are supported by the state. The segregation of wards and the underlying tunnel systems ensures that your family member will never be exposed to someone of a different class level or mix with those of more dangerous afflictions.

–Promotional Material for The Northern Michigan Insane Asylum, 1915

We have been notified that there has been a breakdown of the tunneling system. Several patients have gone missing from locked wards and have been located in the caverns of the facility. We assure the board that this matter has been dealt with efficiently and promptly. All escaped inmates have been found and reassigned. The rumors currently circulating in the Traverse City community are without validity. As you know, with the recent influx of patients, we are experiencing a shortage of beds and materials. We graciously request additional support in both remedial staff and in two to four more physicians so that we can ensure all patients are accounted for at all times. The issue of the tunnels has been addressed and is currently being mended.

—A letter to the Board of Trustees dated 1931

EIGHT

The next morning, Kinney was up before Mallie Lyn Peters could knock on the door.

"I'm sorry to disturb you, sir," she began, then seeing him fully dressed and seated on the bed, "Why! You're an early riser, aren't you? I stopped by the kitchen for some bread for you sir, if you want, and this time I remembered. I told that rascal Charlie—I mean—Mister Young to not disturb me, and I had a purpose. Mr. Young said I, I've got . . . " Mallie's hand went to her mouth again, a look of horror spreading its wings over her face. "Oh, sir. I clean forgot the bread. I went on so much about Mr. Young disturbing me from my purpose that I clean forgot I meant to get you some bread! Would you like me to go back?"

"What I would like, Miss Peters," he said, using her formal name to slow her down and draw her attention, "What I would like is to be taken into the tunnels."

Mallie did not breathe and the natural rose of her cheeks withered. "I'm not sure I understand, sir. Today you're to be meeting with the Board again."

"I've had enough meetings. It is time for me to get to work. It is time for me to do the job they brought me here to do, and that is to tend to the distorted minds that are brought into this facility. Now, if you would kindly take me to the tunnels, *please.*" He issued the 'please' as a command and Mallie Lyn understood it as such.

"The Tunnels," she said softly. She said the phrase as if it was a name, and Kinney understood that here, it was. "They're meant only to take us between buildings sir, when the weather is rough, or someone is very . . . ill . . . and needs to be taken swiftly to the infirmary, or, of course when . . . There isn't anyone down there for you. Your patients are housed in a separate facility, and I can walk you across the courtyard if you would like to get there sooner."

Kinney studied Mallie's face. *There are depths to her, too.* She appeared innocent and girlish and yet, there was an element of steel to her. Did she, like a knife, have a blade?

"You may take me to my office, but I should like to go via The Tunnels." This time he called it by its name instead of saying the words as a descriptor.

"Very well," Mallie said and curtsied, but the way she said it made it very clear to Kinney that all was *not* very well.

51

"But if you don't mind, sir, it won't be me taking you down there. It's not . . . it's not a place for someone like me."

Kinney did not hear Harvey Briggart approach, but rather felt his shadow in the doorway. "If you'll come with me, Doctor Kinney. I will show you the way." Harvey stretched out his hand, as large as a paddle, and Kinney took the first step out of his room and into the sunlight.

NINE

Kinney followed Briggart out of the facility, down a gravel-covered hill, and to a brick entrance hidden by vines. He parted the vines with his massive hands, exposing a large rusted gate. "It looks like the mouth of Hell, doesn't it?" he said, his voice reverberating in Kinney's bones. Briggart withdrew a skeleton key from his pocket and unlocked the gate.

Kinney hesitated before stepping across the threshold. Entrances were also exits. What kind of creatures spewed from its gullet? The thought left him as soon as he heard his name, only the voice speaking to him was not the bass of Briggart, but a voice he knew well and now heard only in his dreams. "Elly!" she called. He shook his head as if to say to the voice, not now.

As soon as they entered the Tunnels, the voice came closer, the voice of a memory, but very present.

Elly, listen to me. I love you. There is nothing wrong with love! A sister can love a brother, and I love you. I love you even with all of the things you've said and done. Who else do we have but each other? Don't look at me! Don't! Take a step back, Elliott, or I swear I'll . . .

Rose's words radiated throughout his body as he stepped into The Tunnels. Harvey's voice pulled him back.

"There are several entrances to the system, and a few we didn't know about until recently. Inmates used them, but I soon put a stop to that. We're under Building 50 now. Follow me." As they trudged forward, Harvey continued to explain about the several entrances throughout the property, mostly camouflaged to blend in with the environment. One entrance could be accessed from Building 50, but it required climbing down a ladder and passing by the refuse containers.

Kinney stepped deeper into the darkness. It smelled, as he expected, of damp earth. But there was something else too. Something foul. Something beyond the remnants of refuse they transported through the tunnels.

Kinney thought again of Rose. How, near the end of her illness she had a similar scent: one of a caged animal.

"I'll lead the way," Harvey said, and Kinney nodded, following him.

The tunnel was wide and tall, as if a gigantic earthworm burrowed beneath and left a cavern in its wake. Brick lined the walls, and they dripped with condensation. With each step Kinney took into the underbelly of the facility, he felt as if he walked back in time, somehow impossibly taking a step closer to Rose.

Love me, she'd cried that final day, pleading, on her knees. *I do love you,* he'd said. *I promised to take care of you, and that's what I'm doing. What more can you want from me?* She looked at him, and he saw it in her eyes. A demon, twisting. It was an abomination. She was a monstrosity. She had the power of demons and had altered his moral sense of decency in a moment of weakness. *Love me the way I want you to* she'd cried. *The way you've done in the dark,* and he had said no. Just one word. Just one word, and it was as if he had unlocked the final door of her madness.

What was it about being here in the Tunnels that brought her so very close to him? Her illness had begun simply enough. She'd always had a dreamy quality to her, but it was that very distance to her, as if she saw into another world just beyond his reach, that he had found so desperately attractive. She'd seemed to belong both of his world and a place where everything was brighter and more beautiful, even after their parents had died in the boating accident. Even after that, when Kinney took care of her, she still smiled and laughed, as if not fully aware they were now alone.

She used to joke she could hear music playing wherever she went, and he had laughed at her, thinking she talked with poetry. Then she'd begun to hear voices talking to her, telling her to do things. He'd thought that by studying *dementia praecox* he'd easily be able to cure her. He had been wrong. One day, he'd returned from the infirmary to find her standing at the kitchen sink, her hands bloodied and still holding the clumps of brown hair she'd ripped from her own scalp. *It's the music,* she'd said. *I've been trying to get it out.* At that moment he knew she'd slipped away from him, and he'd shut his heart to her. He thought his sister a rare beauty to be protected and watched over; she had transformed into a beast and had to be hidden away.

The Tunnels reminded Kinney of his late sister. Not that they were twisted and dark and scary, but if Rose now existed in another plane, it was not someplace magical, but someplace evil like these tunnels. Hadn't she been evil, after all? Hadn't all her talk and laughter and lilting pleas really just been a cover to the blackness of her soul: a blackness that wanted and desired with fire hot intensity? Kinney shivered, and thought of the slender slope of her neck.

His weakness for her was her fault. She'd poisoned him and twisted his own natural yearning as a man for a woman. *No one will know, Elly. Turn out the light. No one will know. I'll never speak of it.*

Harvey Briggart walked briskly in front of him, at first just a pace or two ahead, but soon stretching the space between them that, if it were a rope, it could snap in two. Harvey darted deftly around puddles and cracked bricks, while Kinney's ankle twisted, his feet ill-prepared for this kind of footing.

"Watch your step now, Doctor Kinney," Harvey called, his words echoing. "We're almost to your place."

"Briggart, slow down!" Kinney said and, Harvey paused, allowing him to catch up.

Kinney gulped for air, a waterless fish. "Could you. Explain about. The Tunnels. A bit please. Of the truth." Kinney expected the man to give another version of the tour he'd already received, but this time he'd tell the truth. Truth Kinney suspected. He'd been given the sanitized tour of the facility. They were keeping things from him. Hiding patients from him. They'd cleaned thoroughly, anticipating his arrival. Later, after he'd signed away his life to be employed by them, only then would he see the reality of the place.

Harvey did not give him a tour. He moved his head ever so slightly, which Kinney deciphered as a 'no'. They resumed their walk through the belly of the asylum, Harvey steadily increasing speed until he was a bent shadow just out of reach.

Kinney spun. Certain he'd heard his name. No. A trick. An auditory hallucination, brought on by darkness. But then *Daahhhhkkkterrrrrr Kinnnnnnnneeeeeey* it breathed, soft, barely audible, as if the earth sighed. His name became a loop, one syllable followed by its twin by its twin and its twin, until his name became a horrible twisted sound of an echo turned against itself. He stopped in the tunnel, his heart beating so hard it seemed to want to careen from his chest. He tried to call out to Harvey, to make him stop, but he had no voice. He reached out to steady himself against the wall and touched not the wet, cold surface of stone, but the thick damp mass of a tangle of hair.

TEN

He was upside down. Surely he was upside down!

But, no. That wasn't right. He wasn't floating above the floor, staring at it beneath him. He stared at the ceiling . . . and Mallie Lynn Peters dabbed his forehead with a damp cloth. "There, there, now, Doctor Kinney. It's all right. It's all right now."

He felt, rather than saw, the hulking presence of Briggart leave the room. Mallie continued. "You tripped and fell in the tunnels, you did. Bumped your head good and deep now, didn't you. Afraid there are stitches. But don't you worry. We've done them before. They ain't pretty, but they'll heal. Now, sit up, Doctor Kinney. It's time to start your day." Mallie helped him to a sitting position then offered her arm to steady him as he rose to his feet.

"But there was someone in the Tunnels . . . " he
began. He remembered it clearly. He'd reached out, felt the
tangle of hair, and heard his name echoing around him,
through him. And hadn't he . . . hadn't he seen Rose? Hadn't
he seen Rose standing next to him, her eyes a flash of wild
blue in the darkness, like flint lighting?

"Course there was someone in the Tunnels. There's
always staff in the Tunnels. It's how we get around so
quietly." Mallie studied him, wiped the dirt from his knees
and stepped back. "Now, don't you look a sight, but there's
no more time to waste. Are you ready?"

"Ready for what?" he asked, still confused as to how
he'd ended up in his office and received stitches without
being aware of it.

"It's time to work," Mallie said with more than a hint
of authority in her voice. "Follow me." She turned and exited
the room.

Kinney follow her, but before doing so, he pulled a
single strand of dark hair from his lapel. It was a small thing
but proof enough he'd seen someone in the Tunnels,
someone who worn her hair down, not clasped tightly under
a hat the way support staff did. No. That someone was either
a patient or perhaps . . . perhaps . . .

Kinney shook his head and took after Mallie. He'd
had the slightest moment where he'd actually believed the
woman he'd seen had really been Rose. She had the same
dark hair, the same length, and the same blue eyes that stared
straight into his soul—if, indeed, he still possessed one.

59

*

They walked a short distance to the women's ward. At last, Kinney had a sense of the Northern Michigan Insane Asylum as it really was: a vast machine for the mentally broken, a place inhabited and thriving with a swarm of lost souls. They passed inmates, obvious in their striped pajamas and slippers, walking the grounds. Some exhibited psychoses clearly, while others stared at him a bit too long, their heads cocked a bit too far. Mallie, for once, did not chat too him about bread or Mr. Young. She walked briskly across the courtyard and into the cold, hard building of the women's ward.

"You are to check on patients in Ward B. You're lucky though, Doctor Kinney, Ward B is a pay ward, not the best one though, but at least you're not in the other."

Kinney nodded. There were several areas in the hospital, patients separated first by sex and then by finances. Those with families, who could afford to, paid for their keeping. These inmates were treated to a spacious, open ward and meals that ranged from ham with breakfast to a full dinner at night. Their room was open and peaceful. Inmates were allowed to bring elements from home. That was the highest tier. The second tier belonged to inmates whose families could not afford to keep them in comfort; so they paid a minimal fee to at least ensure that they had decent meals and were tended to with respect. Their room, also wide and open, had more beds in it and no elements of the home.

They had porridge for breakfast, boiled meat, soup. This would be the ward he would attend to.

And finally there was the Ward of the State. These were patients whose families could not pay, did not want to pay, or for inmates who did not have families at all. These were the inmates picked off from the streets and shipped to the asylum so that society would not have to see the effects of long-term syphilis on the brain, or psychoses where someone existed physically in this world, but spiritually they were somewhere or someone else. Kinney and Mallie passed this ward. He heard the women inside, crying, laughing, and shouting. One glance inside the room told him what he had feared. With the economy collapsing, more and more individuals slipped into madness, and no one could afford to pay. The hundred beds were filled in Ward C, and a hundred more women sat, stood and paced in the room. They were fed porridge and a watery soup and when they became very sick, the staff shipped them to another secret room in hopes that their illness would claim them quickly. The State did not like to pay for their upkeep.

"We're here," Mallie said and opened the door to Ward B.

ELEVEN

He had expected to walk in, sit quietly at a desk, observe then leave. Kinney should learn that life never operates the way you expect. It's as if, as soon as you form an expectation, life hears you and makes a different choice just to spite you.

Kinney walked into a large room with a few tables and chairs and wide windows. The windows were barred, and the shadows cut crosses along the marbled floor. Mallie passed him a file, and the women surged forward.

The room shrunk to the size of a broom closet. He tried to walk forward. Tried to breathe. Tried to keep his gaze firmly in front of him. He was a tall man and the women reached up to him. He registered their touching his shoulders, his neck, and his hair not as individual women, but as if a mythical creature with a hundred arms and a thousand probing tendrils accosted him.

"Line up!" Mallie Lynn cried, her voice showing more than that hint of steel. "It's Doctor Kinney to examine you!"

She stomped her foot against the tile, and the room fell to a hush. The wave of hands reaching to feel him ebbed, and the women parted. A tiny, old woman stood before him. Her unsecured gray hair fell to the middle of her torso and wrapped her small frame like a shawl.

"You've been in The Tunnels, you have," she whispered, her voice like an injection of ice to his veins. "You'll be back there, too. Once The Tunnels touches you, you're never the same." She pointed to him, and he tentatively touched the stitches that stretched across his face.

Mallie looked at Kinney and said softly, "Her name is Mrs. Grant, sir. We don't ever use her first name, sir, not ever. She bites." Mallie placed a file in Kinney's hands.

He began his work.

TWELVE

That night, he sat in his room, the world moaning outside his window. Snow was in the air, and the coming of ice seemed to whisper and crawl under the door and into his very bones. It shook the bare trees and rattled the windowpanes. Kinney drew his robe around him, sat at his desk, and opened his precious bag that contained his research. He did not think of the waves of patients he'd spoken with and analyzed. He did not replay assigning therapies, addressing issues, discussing treatment plans. He did not look to tomorrow when he would finally—at long last—oversee the hydrotherapy sessions. He did not revisit his ideas and plans for new therapies or read any of the published journals that discussed experiments with brain tissue and how elimination of key areas of the brain could cure a patient of all psychoses . . . and perhaps all emotion as well.

No.

He did not think of these things.

He lay in bed and listened to the moans of wind, which might actually have been the crying out of patients trapped in diseased minds. He thought of Rose, singing to him. If he focused, he could hear her singing even now, her voice as far away as memory, and as soft as a promise. As he drifted to sleep he thought, for a moment, that her song came from somewhere beneath him, directly under him. Perhaps, straight from the Tunnels.

He shook the thoughts from him, as if shaking off rainwater. He must focus on his work. In his work, there was safety. He began to re-read his notes.

The words blurred. Sound faded. Thoughts of Rose surfaced. Rose was in every memory he had. There were so few of his parents, either because they had died when he was seventeen, or because his sister had so seamlessly replaced them. Rose, always there, to comfort him, care for him. She was a soft touch on his shoulder while he studied, encouragement when he needed it, a sandwich prepared for him and left by his side when he'd been so absorbed in his work he'd forgotten to eat. Wasn't that love? A sister's love for her brother had a kind of purity to it, didn't it?

Then it twisted. Darkened. There were too many hours spent alone with her. He'd not set up the proper boundaries. He should have found a husband for her as soon as he could. The light touch on his neck lingered a bit too long, her parted lips, a flick of her pink tongue, her fingers tracing the curve of her neck as she brushed a strand of hair out of her face and tucked it behind her ear.

No. This was not a sister's love for her brother.

She was a witch. A curse! His sister's love for him was an abomination, and he must not think of her lips or the smell of her hair.

He worked. He began with the first entry, his idea on rebuilding someone's personality, of injecting memories and ideas into their very spirit. He'd been cursed with his soul mate in the wrong human form. And what was a soul, but thoughts, ideas, and memories? If he could, he would transplant those things into another human form—and in this way, he could bring Rose back to him. This time he could love her without shame. He could kiss her lips, her soft neck, and the swell of her breasts. He could take her as his, and this time, he could keep her.

With these thoughts, and Rose's song calling to him, he worked through the night.

THIRTEEN

From the deepest shadows, the young woman watched the man work until nearly dawn when he surrendered and collapsed in bed, asleep but not resting. His dark hair fell across his eyes and his chest rose and fell with each breath. He looked sad, even sleeping. She reached out her hand to touch him and, gently as a whisper, touched his brow. Even sleeping, he looked different than the others. She drew her head back and studied him.

"Alma, no!" we hissed.

The woman heard her name and withdrew, sinking into the night. She knew the truth, but we still reminded her. She was not to touch this man. Not this one. He was of the upper world. He was not a Tunnel Person. He would not understand her. She knew this. She felt it as a truth.

"But he's so beautiful," she said.

"No" we answered her, and thought it was enough.

Even as Alma followed one of us back down into the Tunnels, she knew without question she would be back, and next time she would touch his lips.

FOURTEEN

It was 1911

We took the baby in our arms.

"She's a she," Liliana said and immediately wrapped the baby in hospital rags and began to wipe the effluvia of birth from the baby's wrinkled face. Beeler's white hand reached out and touched the mother's face. He made birds with his hands and motioned that they'd flown away. He'd long ago bitten off his own tongue, rendering him mute.

"Yes, Beeler," Kostic said. "She's dead. This thing has killed her. I knew it'd kill her. Demons exploding from her stomach like that. I'll take care of it. I'll smother it. I'll use my bare hands." His muscles shivered in anticipation.

Lynnie Grant shuffled forward. Even at fifty, her dowager's hump had bent her into a sharp hook, causing her to crane her face to look at you.

"You will not touch the child," she said to Kostic, pointing a long finger at him. "She's been sent to us from Above." Lynnie pointed to the ceiling of the Tunnel, and we all knew that she wasn't talking about God. This baby was half a Tunnel Person, and half from the land of Above. She'd been sent to us as a link.

The four of us began to speak in excited whispers. We'd known something was brewing, and we'd waited desperately for a sign. Then it happened.

"Poor little one wants to suckle," Liliana said and untied her white gown to expose a pert breast, its nipple ready.

Kostic flicked her hand away. "Put that away, woman. You've nothing in you to give that demon."

"I will make milk. My love for her will make it happen." She cuddled the child against her chest.

The albino Beeler grunted. He grabbed a piece of chalk and wrote on the wall and we waited as we listened to the chalk crawl across the surface. SHE IS OURS. WE WILL RAISE HER. THE 4 OF US.

Kostic laughed. We waited to see if he would snap, as he was wont to do at times. His anger seethed like a viper just below the surface of his skin, but you could sometimes see it coiling.

"Give her to me," he said.

Liliana stared into his eyes and refused to back down. He could snap her in two and toss her aside, yet she did not give in. Then her eyes began to flutter, and we knew what was coming. She began to shake as the earth does when its separate pieces collide.

In a flash, Kostic reached for the child before Liliana collapsed to the floor, her body wracked with the seizures that at times overtook her.

"If you harm that baby . . ." Lynnie began.

Kostic stared at the small child in his arms. She was as frail as an icicle. Her tiny face scrunched and mewed like a kitten. He could snuff out her life as easily as a candle flame, but instead, something in him shifted. He heard the voices as if they came from a radio, though it was only broadcast in his mind. "You will protect her . . ." they said.

"We will raise her," Kostic at last agreed. "All of us."

We agreed in silence, and waited for Liliana's body to be still. At last, she rested peacefully at our feet. Beeler and Lynnie Grant helped her to sit up.

"I've had a vision," Liliana said softly. "We will name her Alma."

"Alma," Kostic agreed.

"It means 'soul'."

In that moment, we decided. She was ours. Our Alma. Whatever was left of our souls in this place, she would carry within her. Together we would shelter her, find her food, and protect her with our very lives, if needed.

For twenty years, this is exactly what we did.

Then Alma, our beautiful Alma, met Dr. Kinney, and for the first time, we knew real fear.

FIFTEEN

At last, Doctor Kinney was working, doing the things he'd been hired to do: assess patients, prescribe treatments, and administer treatments. After a month at the institution, he could finally navigate the hallways without getting lost, though he still had Mallie Lynn Peters escort him to the ladies' ward, or he followed behind Briggart to other parts of the facility.

Kinney felt as if he lived two lives at the Northern Michigan Insane Asylum. During the day, he donned his white coat and observed patients and dictated to nurses and orderlies what they should do to control and quiet the inmates. He'd finally been granted access to the lowest level of the facility and could finally work on treating the most diseased minds, something he found extremely interesting.

At night, he left disease and darkness, and slipped into a crisp suit to join high-ranking members of the staff for elegant dinners in the dining room with silver service, crystal glasses, and four course meals, all served by inmates. Several female inmates tended to them in the smoking room when the wives had retired. Interred at the asylum for reasons of promiscuity, the inmates tended to the gentlemen in ways Kinney found abhorrent. In general, the inmates functioned in everyday life as long as you did not look too deeply into their eyes and risk the siren's call.

In the smoking room, many of the doctors did not resist them; in fact, they seemed to actively seek them out. Kinney kept his eyes averted and returned to his room and research as soon as he could do so without looking like he disapproved of his colleagues' behavior.

In this way, Kinney's days and evenings marched on.

October passed quietly and slipped into November. Kinney's days began to replicate; he began to have trouble discerning one from the next. His days fell into a pattern and only his schedule helped him tell them apart. He was grateful for this predictability. He breathed easier as he became trapped in the tumble of repetition, and his past slipped farther and farther away.

Sundays were rest days for him and the staff. On Sundays, inmates were essentially left on their own, locked in their wards. They did not mill the campus, but sat in their beds or in rocking chairs or paced inside their wards.

Mondays were difficult because the inmates had regressed into their illnesses from a day of neglect. Kinney believed, as did the staff, that the diseased mind flourished in solitude. Only through work could demons be quieted. On Mondays, he conducted therapy sessions of hydrotherapy and colonics.

State asylums started using a new treatment called insulin shock therapy. Large doses of insulin were injected into the inmate to induce a coma. This relaxed the brain and allowed the patient time to rest and heal. Too much insulin could cause death, so while Kinney liked the idea of the therapy, he felt more confident with older, practiced remedies. Hydrotherapy sessions seemed to offer the most benefit as the hours emerged in cold water or shooting water into a patient's face shocked the mind into lucidity, however briefly. As Kinney watched one of the patients thrash in the water, he thought that nearly dying must be a transformative event. To be just on the brink, teetering between existence and blackness . . . surely that experience would transform you.

Tuesdays, Wednesdays and Saturdays, he visited each ward and marked off charts. Thursdays, he attended meetings with the board and other staff members. Fridays had been set aside for research, and he looked forward to this day beyond all others, the day just beyond his reach. He had freedom on Fridays. He could walk the grounds and find solace in the comfort of his own mind. On Fridays, he would read the latest scientific journals and work on his own ideas. Neurosurgery and removing diseased portions of the brain to heal a person fascinated him. He had, in his previous position, attempted such an operation, but the results of the experiment had been, sadly, fatal. Still, Kinney felt as if he'd brought the patient peace. His mind, while no longer existing, was at least free of conflict and disorder. It was, in essence, free of everything.

The Board slowly left him alone and Kinney attended the long dinners and smoking sessions less and less, until finally, he could move about the asylum quietly and conduct the research that interested him the most. Diseased minds, by their very sickness, were pliable.

During sessions with patients, he experimented with memory suggestion. He'd had the idea that maybe he could change a person's personality by providing them with an alternate history. Their minds were so pliable, so open to suggestion, that he instilled in a few patients the childhood memories of a puppy named Chocolate, strangled by their father in front of their four-year-old eyes.

It was a simple experiment, but did not quite satisfy him. One memory was a parlor trick. The real trick would be to obliterate one's foundation and replace it with a new one. Kinney tried not to think of this. He had other work to do; work he must complete to leave him free for his own interests.

He grabbed his notebook and decided to visit the men's ward for his research today, taking a shortcut through the Tunnels. The Tunnels called him—quite literally. At night he would awaken in his bed, shivering with a cold sweat, and he would swear he heard Rose call his name. He resisted walking in the Tunnels because he was afraid what might happen to him. Yes, he was afraid.

On this Friday, though, the Tunnels would be required. It was November, and the grounds were barren and cold, twisted tree limbs reached out in agony. An ice storm brewed and the trees moaned with the weight of their burden. Kinney looked behind him to make sure he was not being followed and slipped silently below ground.

SIXTEEN

The rain started in the afternoon, a heavy rain on the verge of turning to ice. Kinney entered the Tunnels from the staff entrance. It was not a pleasant way to go as the staff used it to transport refuse out of the facility, and the stink of the room turned his stomach. Still, this way he could avoid going outside into the storm. Lately, he'd been fighting a cold and a slight fever and did not want to add to his illness by catching a chill.

Kinney unlocked the grate in the floor, lifted it with a clang, then climbed down using the cool ladder, slippery and unpleasant under his palms. Garbage was lowered by a pulley system and scraps of food slipped under his feet as he touched the floor. Over time, he had learned the twists and turns of the Tunnels so they were no longer quite so labyrinth. If he went down, right, then right again, he'd come to the secret Ward E, the empty prison-like room outfitted with a deep tub and other equipment he used for hydrotherapy sessions. Ward E also held several cells for the criminally insane, kept there until they could be transferred elsewhere, or put in a cell for punishment. Only one room was currently occupied, by the particularly violent character Robert Kostic.

Kostic's muscles rippled like a stallion's, and he had the look in his eye of a viper about to strike. Kinney was determined to break his spirit, cleansing him of demonic forces. He'd prescribed a series of hydrotherapy sessions so intense, Kostic appeared at times to hang on the cliff of death, but somehow he always fought back to consciousness.

Kinney did not visit him tonight, though.

Tonight, he'd come for himself—for in the Tunnels, he felt closest to Rose.

She called to him. Kinney did not believe in ghosts. He knew her voice was as real as his own; it was time to call the demon out.

SEVENTEEN

He was deep in the belly of the Tunnels when he heard a great boom aboveground. He heard the crack of wood that could only be a tree falling, perhaps giving in to the weight of the ice. The lights in the tunnels flickered and went out.

Kinney did not move. He knew if he waited and controlled his breathing, his irises would adjust to the new darkness. In moments, the darkness would lighten, turn purple, and he would be able to see. He must not panic.

The dark was immense. Terrifying. His heart thrummed. He must not panic!

He heard footsteps. Something shuffling. A laugh. Behind him? He turned. No. In front of him. To the side of him.

"Who are you?" he called, his voice echoing around him.

Whoareyouwhouareyouwhoareyou bounced to him, the words whispered and layered, and Kinney was certain it was not his own voice coming back at him.

"I have a gun!" he called then instantly felt foolish. Yelling at shadows. And of course, he did not have a gun.

After a moment, he realized the phrase "I have a gun" did not return to him. There was silence. Then something clanked. Something *slithered.*

He began to see. Just shadows at first. He made out a dim light in the distance. And then, to his growing horror, he realized those shadows in front of him moved. One scurried on the ground, a lump . . . a moving lump the size of a person on their knees. Two to the side, the shadows as tall as Briggart. Kinney spun. Two more shadows moved toward him . . . one slender and jumping, the next moving fluidly as if gliding on air.

The gliding shadow asked him softly, the voice lyrical, "Who are you?" and grabbed his face with cold fingers as comforting as talons. "Who are you?" The woman whispered again, for it was a woman, and her voice in the darkness was as melodic as a lullaby. She leaned in close to him, pressed her nose against his neck and . . . sniffed. When she drew her face back to look at him, Kinney lost his tender hold on panic.

He looked into the face of his Rose, his dear sister, dead for three years.

"You know me," he managed, barely able to form the words. "You call me Elly."

She looked at him. Cocked her head.

"El-Lee," She said, but it was Rose, wasn't it? It was Rose, his beloved dead sister, risen from the grave, or halfway from the grave and existing in the in-between of the Tunnels. She was here to forgive him. Rose! Back from the dead!

And yet—no. She was not Rose.

The woman was young, twenty or so, with long dark hair and pale skin. She was, without question, beautiful, like a delicate trillium. She resembled his sister in coloring, but that was all. His sister was still in the grave.

"Meet my family," she said softly. She gestured to the other shadows, and Kinney turned his eyes toward them. He could see them now as four distinct people, two men and two women. His heart stopped in his chest. They were inmates, surely, inmates loose in the Tunnels, inmates with bloodied feet and dirty pajamas, with eyes fueled by disease and torment. He recognized one, a man lean with muscles sharpened by hard work.

"Kinney!" Kostic hissed.

"Kinney!" the others echoed.

Then they were upon him.

EIGHTEEN

Images came to Kinney in waves, violent as the lake in a storm. He stood in the cell, Kostic floating before him in the tub. Ice water rushed over Kinney's hands as he pressed against Kostic's lean, muscled chest. With a firm push downward, Kinney forced him under the water and held. Two orderlies stood by, ready to assist, but he liked to do this work himself. Kostic thrashed, churning the water like a great sea beast. Kinney held. The water was so cold he soon lost any feeling at all in his arms and this comforted him. Kostic thrashed and thrashed until power surged into Kinney's hands and up his arms . . .

Then Kinney walked barefoot on a beach, studying the sands in search of Petoskey stones, fossils that would not show themselves unless touched by water. The sand was almost too hot against his toes. His cold arm ached, as if he still held Kostic underwater. He turned the sand with his bare toes searching, but found nothing. Then, out in the water, a flash of white caught his eye. Perhaps the crest of a wave mounting? No. Not a wave at all. No.

It was Rose, floating in the lake by their house, fully clothed, her white dress spilling around her, her hair reaching out and bleeding with the water. Kinney called to her.

"Rose! Rose, come back!" He charged into the water, and the undertow pulled at his legs as fierce as if Poseidon yanked his feet . . .

He was sucked under water, but he was no longer in the lake. No. He lay naked in a tub, his chest the color of a bloated fish, and Kostic stood above him. Kostic laughed as he pushed Kinney under . . .

That was all a dream though, wasn't it? Kinney was not underwater. He was not in a tub, but on the ground, flat on his back. Water dripped from the Tunnel's walls. He was breathing. A man with long white hair leaned over him and put his head to his heart. White hair? Yes. And the pale eyes of an albino—his skin the color of a ghost. He wrote something on a tablet and held it out to the others.

"Sick like us?" Asked an old woman.

"No. He's a doctor. He's one of *them*." Answered a lovely woman with large breasts in a too-tight top. She licked her lips. "Get away get away don't touch don't touch." Fingers tickled him. "I'll touch him. Get him. Taste him." The fingers pulled back, and Kinney's arm warmed. There was pressure, too, and he realized someone held onto him.

Rose looked down at him, touched his forehead, her smile deep with sympathy. "Poor baby," she said. "Poor baby." She kissed him lightly on the lips, her touch cool.

Someone sang, softly at first, and with growing force, as if he walked closer to the source of the voice. But he was not walking, was he? The sound carried him. Mallie. Mallie Lyn Peters sang a lullaby to him. The voices called to him. Mallie's voice and Rose's beautiful and harmonizing, but the others . . . the others delayed and discordant and sharp as razors.

Rose looked at him. His Rose. "Poor baby," she said, and she kissed him again, her lips sweeter than he remembered. She tasted of honey.

Rays of light and shadows shifted and oozed and took human shape. Hands grabbed him, dug into his shoulders and waist, and lifted him. He was carried, floated through the air, tumbled without touching the ground. He could not scream. He could not talk. Someone had stolen his voice, his very breath.

It was a dream. Of course he dreamed, but he was also half-awake. He floated in the netherworld between the dream state and reality and could not cross over. When Kinney finally woke, rain thrashed the windows. An ice storm. Someone choked, and he slowly realized it was himself.

"You've had a fever, Doctor Kinney," Mallie murmured to him. "Take a deep breath now. You're all right. All is well. You are well now. You collapsed you did. Underneath."

Kinney tried to speak but his voice was hoarse and not his own.

Mallie nodded as if she understood. "How long were you down there? You were missing for a time. Overnight maybe? Chilled, feverish. Then you were helped up here, and I've been taking care of you ever since. It's been a week now. We thought we'd lose you, but Alma said no. You were a fighter, and Alma is one to know."

"Alma?" It was the only word he could manage to speak clearly.

Mallie Lyn leaned in close to him and whispered in his ear. "She's a secret, Doctor Kinney. One you must keep. Please, sir. If you could."

He nodded his head and noticed Alma in the room. She sat in the corner, her face hidden in shadow, but clearly the mirror image of Rose. Kinney was not a religious man, but at once he believed in a power greater than himself. He nodded again, and Alma rose from her chair to come to him.

"Yes," he said. He would promise to keep her.

Alma stepped into the light. "Hello, Elly," she said softly and reached to touch his face.

He burned. Suddenly. Fiercely. And with a different kind of fever. She was Rose and not-Rose, but without question, Kinney knew one thing: this Alma would belong to him. He would own her. Completely.

"Hello, again," he said.

He slipped back into sleep but this time, he did not dream.

NINETEEN

Alma began to go to him then. We warned her, told her no, told her he was one of Them and to be feared.

"But I'm drawn to him," she said. "There's something pulling me to him. I must go."

At first we tried to stop her. We threatened. We pulled on her. "Do not go!" we hissed. Mama Liliana told her stories of the evil that men do. "He'll impale you with his thing. He'll take away your soul with it. Leave you battered and swollen and wanting more."

Alma laughed at her. "I know that isn't true, Mama Liliana. You've told me many times how to enjoy a man. How to control him. I know how to do it."

"He tortures us!" Mama Grant said, trying to crane her neck upward to look at her. "Look at what he's done to my back. HE did this. Bent me over! Forced me frozen!"

"He did no such thing. Your own spine has bent you forward, not anything the doctors have done. I know what they do," Alma continued. *"I've watched them my whole life. I've read their books. They do try to help, and for the most part they get it right. They just don't know how to talk to you the way I do."* She brushed her hands through her dark hair, and we listened. We knew she was right. Alma understood us. Not just the four of us, but all the inmates. At night, she would slip into locked wards and comfort those of us who needed her. She could look at an inmate and know what words to say, how to navigate the way their minds functioned. She could soothe, talk down, and be firm as needed. But no one had interested her the way Kinney did.

"I've been following him since he got here," she said although we already knew. And we knew that she risked more. At night, she'd sometimes watch him sleep. Once, she reached out and touched the curve of his chin. *"There's something there,"* she said. *"Something between us that is different than with any of you."*

We could not talk her out of it. We could not stop her. We knew what was different between them. It was a thread stretching to bind them together. White ribbon on Alma's side; black rope on Kinney's. You cannot stop souls who reach out to each other, even if you know that tie will ensnare one of them. You cannot stop love, even if it is the dark kind. Especially if it is the dark kind.

And so we vowed to continue to watch over her.

Perhaps she could take what she wanted from Kinney for a while. Once she'd had her fill, she could leave him empty. It could be enough to destroy him, send him packing, and above all we wanted him out. We saw the books he read, the tools he'd begun to practice

87

with. It was only a matter of time before he started trying to take out illnesses with an ice pick. He saw minds as tortured and diseased; we saw minds as they were: a varied and beautiful kind of magic. Perhaps Alma's love for him could deter him from that dark path. And then once removed, perhaps that love could crush him.

We turned to Liliana. Liliana knew how to handle a man. Kostic and Beeler would not give instruction. They turned their backs on it. But Liliana could coach her on how to control and protect herself from pain. How to take pleasure from the man until she'd had her fill, then she could abandon him.

TWENTY

"You've had a fever, you have sir," said Mallie Lynn, sponging his forehead. "Dr. Grooms says it's not uncommon when new physicians come and work here. There's so much sickness in the air, it seems right you would catch it."

Kinney nodded and sat up in bed. "How long this time?"

"Just a day and night. You're feeling better though?"

"Much," he said.

"Good then. I'll go and get you some soup. Dr. Grooms says if you're up to it you can make your rounds tomorrow sir, but you're to rest today."

"Thank you, Mallie." The girl blushed to the root of her red hair then curtsied, exiting his room quickly.

Kinney forced himself out of bed. He smelled of sweat and sleep. He must clean himself and be more presentable for when Mallie returned. Already he must appear weak to the staff. It wouldn't do to lose their respect so soon after arriving. He had so much work to do, and much of it required the willingness of the support staff to look the other way.

He wore a gown similar to the inmates'. He tore it off and stood naked in the cold room. He reached for the pot of water by his dresser, dipped the washcloth in, wrung it out, and began to scrub at his skin.

Something touched his back. A feather. A tickle. Something soft. He spun around, nearly knocking the woman over. Rose stood before him. No. Not Rose. Alma. The young woman from the Tunnels.

"What the devil!" he cried and quickly covered his genitals with the cloth.

She smiled at him, a smile that hinted at knowing what a man could want. "Shh," she said. She was so beautiful. Her skin was flawless and her dark hair hung loose around her face and down her shoulders. She wore a dressing gown so gossamer he could see the outline of her breasts, the curve of her hips. "Let me," she offered.

She took the washcloth from him.

Kinney did not know what to do, so he closed his eyes. He felt her then, touching him. Washing him with the cloth. Her hand dipped in the water. He listened to her squeeze the cloth dry. Heard the water drip into the bowl. Her touch against him was light and delicate, but everywhere her fingers danced, his body responded with a burn, a flame so hot it took his breath from him.

For a moment, with his eyes closed, he could imagine it was his sister. Usually this brought a bout of repulsion and dismay, to think of his sister as a man thinks of a woman. But this, this was not his sister. No one had seen her enter his room. The door was locked. Mallie Lynn might not return for a half hour or so while she prepared his soup.

He opened his eyes.

He reached for her, and wrenched the cloth from her hands. She grabbed for it.

"No," he said, firmly, and he grabbed her arm to stop her. For a moment, they stood like that. He could feel her breathing. His body was cold and wet and hot all at once. He could stand it no longer. He pulled her to him. Hard. This woman who so resembled his soul mate, but had the benefit of not being born from his own parents.

Her breasts flattened against him, and he kissed her, giving in to an ache and a need that came from the darkest corners of his spirit. She met him kiss for kiss, and when he reached to undo the top of her gown, she stepped back, pulled a tie, and exposed the beautiful lithe body that seemed to want as much as he did.

"God," he breathed.

What she did to him next convinced him she was no angel, no heavenly creature, and he surrendered to her dark powers.

TWENTY-ONE

She left him breathless, spent, and tangled in the sheets of his bed.

When Mallie Lynn returned with a tray with soup and bread, she rushed to his side. "Are you worse?" she cried. "Are you feverish"

Kinney only laughed, not knowing if he'd just experienced some kind of waking dream due to fever, or if the succubus was real. "I am ravenous," he said as he took the soup, though it wasn't for food he hungered.

PART THREE – Outside

Letter addressed to Board of Directors, 1912:

There have been rumors circulating the facility that an inmate gave birth to a child in the tunnels. This is a fallacy. Yes, a young woman was found in an exhausted state and she had signs of a physical attack, but she shows no signs of having been pregnant at any time. The woman has been transferred to another location and is recovering. Her family has been informed. The breach in the tunnels has been fixed. Dear fellows, rumors circulate, you must know that. Especially in an asylum for the deranged.

–Signed, Patrick Callahan

Letter addressed to Doctor Grooms, Superintendent, 1912:

I am writing because I cannot live with this secret. You know as well as I do that the woman in question had a child. Where has that child gone? If the child has been taken, it is kidnapping. If the child . . . if the child is dead, then perhaps it is murder. How am I to cover this up? You cannot ask it of me! I no longer wish to be a part of this establishment. I cannot continue in this subterfuge and so I am taking another position. Please allow me a two weeks pay stipend, in return of which, I promise not to speak of this. I have written to the board as you requested, but that is the last of it. I wash my hands of this affair, sir. I beg you never to speak of it to me again.

–Signed, Patrick Callahan

Handwritten note addressed to Dr. Kinney and marked PRIVATE

"There are two people in this room, Doctor. One is sane. One is as crazy as they come. I assure you, sir, I am sane. So which one are you?"

On the walls of the tunnels in green crayon:

A L M A

TWENTY-TWO

The ice storms of November slipped into the soft snowfall of an early winter. The cool, fresh air renewed Kinney. He slept deeply. He woke quickly. His movements took on a vigor he had lacked for many years. When he polished his shoes, the brush snapped across the surface. When he shaved, his blade was quick and did not shake. He walked briskly as if his feet could at any moment propel him into the air. He saw his patients and monitored, tended. He ate lush meals with the Board of Trustees and his fellow doctors. He smiled, laughed, and told them nothing about his secret joy. He found a new way to laugh, deep from his belly. His eyes sparked. And every day he used his energy to propel him into the next moment, the next second, because every second that clicked by was another second closer to seeing his Rose.

Of course, he knew the woman who came to him at night and slipped into his bed was not his sister. He had buried his Rose; seen her eyes sewn shut. But this woman, when she whispered his name, when she kissed him, when he trailed his hands along the curves of her breasts to the flat of her stomach, this woman in the darkness and the quiet might as well have been his sister, but without the irons of shame.

This woman, this Alma, was an echo of his Rose, but lacked the shared blood in his veins. She was free for him to claim, to love openly. Free even to marry. She was his wife in every way but one. She was his wife in the shadows; in the daylight, he was a widower.

Why did she come to him in secret? She was young and beautiful, and there should be no reason for their secrecy. She was not married, and he could find no record of her as an inmate at the asylum. He knew that several of the doctors kept a Ferris wheel of mistresses culled from the inhabitants of these walls.

She would tell him nothing. She knew nothing. "Where were you born?" he asked her one night after making love. Their bodies were warm against the clawing cold of the night air. The soft down on her arm stood with the chill.

"Here," she whispered and then kissed his chest. "And here." She kissed him again.

"Here? You mean here, here at the asylum. But how?" He tried to pull away, but she kissed him again, the side of his neck, his ear.

"Yes, here. Here. Everywhere." She kissed him again, and he lost all sense of himself.

He'd heard rumors, of course. The Trustees and their wives spoke of ghosts; the inmates, though, whispered of a child born in the dark, raised to watch over them and tend to them when the doctors failed. Surely there was no Truth there.

Then he noticed the inmates watching him in a new way. They stared a little too long, let loose a knowing smile, let a hand brush against him in some kind of support or message. He heard whispers. "Dr. Kinney belongs to her. He will watch over us too." But who was she?

He could not let go of not knowing. It ate at him from within.

TWENTY-THREE

"What do you know of her, Mallie?" he asked while following her to visit the women's ward; she was delivering dressings and medicine to one of the nurses.

She hurried away from him. "I don't know anything about Alma," she said, though Kinney had not offered the name. Mallie Lynn refused to say more. "I can't speak of it, sir," she said. And she would not.

Kinney took it upon himself to discover the origin of this woman, a woman of his dreams who came to him at night and loved him fiercely as a succubus then disappeared with the morning. He searched records and files. He dug through other patients' paperwork. And he talked to the patients, probing tenderly with questions to find the truth. What do you know? He'd ask. And sometimes he'd say just

101

her name, just Alma, and see if their eyes flickered. A flicker that said they knew.

He gathered truth like berries. He held them close to him, and in time he discovered the fruit of her story. Alma had been born in the tunnels of the asylum. Her mother was an inmate. She had no parents, no wards, except for the people who visited her and tended to her. There were four patients she looked to as her family, although over the years there had been many others: two mothers, two fathers, all of them, all four of them inmates of the asylum. Alma should be infected, perverse—murderous even, being raised by such a *family* and in such an environment. Nurture, after all, dements nature. And yet . . . Alma was nearly perfect in every way. She seemed not to exhibit any psychosis. How could a child born in an asylum and raised, it seemed, by a collective of lunatics, have survived at all let alone flourished into such a woman? Such a perfect creature?

Kinney could not understand. He wanted to. He wanted to crawl into the tender pieces of her mind to discover the magic of it. How was it possible? It wasn't! But, of course, it was.

Alma was perfect in nearly every way. Her body was lithe and pert, her hair thick and glossy. Her eyes hinted at a keen intelligence and there was a sense of whimsy about her. So nearly perfect, except that she seemed to have no concept of time or place, of memory. She lived fully in the here and now. It could be her undoing. It could be Kinney's way in.

It was this—along with her striking resemblance to Rose—that gave him the idea. If he could implant some memories, if he could change the inflection of words, make her say certain phrases, if he could get her to say to him how much she loved him, the way Rose had said so many times before she slipped away from him . . . wouldn't it be a way of bringing Rose back? Alma was a blank slate, an unshaped personality. She was a child trapped in the body of a woman he loved.

"I can free her. I have the power and the knowledge to do it. She is, after all, not really wholly formed. She is open to suggestion and I could fill her with a past of my choosing."

In his career past, he'd attempted to free lunatics of their diseased spirits by cutting out portions of the brain. To transform Alma would require no surgery, just a steady hand in manipulation, an understanding of the brain and memory. He could do it.

"Alma." He pulled her on top of him. Her smooth skin warmed him. Like this, their bodies pressed tight, there was no space between them. Not even air could separate them. "I want to call you something else. A name. A pet name. A name I will whisper to you, and you will know is yours."

"Yes," she whispered. Her body rocked against him.

"I will call you Rose," he said, and this time *he* kissed *her*. Drank of her. Breathed her in. "Rose," he said again, and feeling the name against his lips allowed him to begin to devour her. He closed his eyes and kissed her deeply, closing his eyes to who she actually was and imagining his Rose returned from the grave, only *this* time he would be allowed to posses her as he wanted. These thoughts aroused in him a fire he had never experienced. He flipped the woman under him, and she opened to him, her laugh tinkling in the night. He silenced her with his tongue. "Rose," he whispered again and again as he dove into her very soul. She cried out in pleasure saying "Yes!" and thus accepted her new identity. She would be his Rose; she would leave Alma behind. The transformation put him over the edge.

Spent, he did not pull away from her, but allowed himself to pulse within her, allowing part of his spirit to merge with hers. Her heavy breathing, her silence accepted him, pulled him in. Then he was lost to all thought . . . at least until the morning dawned.

TWENTY-FOUR

In the morning, Kinney awoke to the emptiness of the bed and his room, and the awareness that to accomplish his goal, he would need to take steps. His work became secondary; his new work–to raise Rose from the dead– possessed him. He could do this. Maybe not in the literal sense, but in a poetic one.

He went through his morning routine first, his body performing the motions, though his mind worked on other things. First steps began with the ritual of shaving. Cold water. Lathering the soap in the cup. Dragging the straight blade down the sharp curve of his jaw. Just a touch of blood. Never mind. There was always a scratch or two when preparing to greet the world. Then the dressing: under garments, starched shirt, dark trousers, shoes polished to a dark mirror. He smoothed pomade in his hair until every hair lay perfectly in place. He thought of how to root Rose out from the shadows and bring her into the light. His feet moved on without him. He did not go to the dining hall for coffee and food to be spooned upon a platter for him. He went quietly down into the tunnels. He too could have a secret hiding spot. Kinney was a quick learner.

As a doctor, Kinney had realized early on that before taking any precipitous steps with a patient, he must observe quietly first. Only after hours of observation, could he know how to remove the cause of his suffering, as one would cut out a cancerous growth. Kinney suffered now. Every moment when his Rose was not with him—for he thought of Alma entirely as *his* Rose now—he suffered gravely. He'd lost weight, the sharp blades of his bones becoming more pronounced. He coughed more, and at times had such trouble breathing he feared he'd faint. When Rose was with him all signs of his illness abated. He was well. He must figure out a way to remove Rose from the darkness of the Tunnels and take her into the light of his own life.

As was his routine, he began to observe from the shadows. Alma, from a distance, looked so much like his Rose. The same dark hair. The same long neck. The same way of brushing her hair. Sometimes, Alma seamlessly became Rose to him, so that he began to confuse their names. An idea formed in Kinney's mind, but first he would need to learn everything he could about this mysterious creature, Alma.

This morning, the albino Beeler attended Alma. The four inmates exhibited vastly different psychoses, and on their own could barely tend to themselves, let alone take care of a child. Collectively, he noted, it was a different story entirely. They helped each other. Where one patient had a weakness, another had strengths.

The albino did not talk, from either a self-imposed silence, or perhaps his albinism was only one tendril of deeper malformations. Perhaps he did not have a tongue with which to speak. Beeler's strength was tending to Alma, protecting her while she slept. He watched over her, fiercely at times. If there were no other noises in the tunnel room where she slept, Beeler drew pictures for her. Her room consisted of a stained mattress and an odd collection of broken toys and dolls on slanted shelves. Alone, the small room would be dismal, but Beeler's drawings had transformed it into a childish paradise. While Beeler was without color, he drew and painted pictures with hues so vibrant they practically vibrated. A deep blue waterfall, and woods so lush it seemed to hum, covered the walls. Butterflies of inexplicable colors flew and hid in flowers. Woodland creatures peered from branches and fields. The cool simple beauty of sister moons circled the ceiling.

Once, Kinney had stifled a cough, and Beeler had immediately turned in place and seemed to stare straight at him. Kinney dared not breathe, especially when a growl of inhuman nature issued from the throat of the albino. Hours passed, seemingly, until Beeler returned to his sketching.

Kinney had no doubt that if the inmate had caught him observing, he might have torn out Kinney's tongue, rendering him without speech, too.

Over time, Kinney had observed the others with her, too. He was surprised to see Kostic as one of her guardians. How did he get free? How did any of them? Kostic was her guardian and storyteller. Kostic suffered from the newly-termed paranoid schizophrenia. He had moments of extreme lucidity, even an otherworldly calm, and moments of extreme violence . . . yet somehow he used this diseased part of his mind to spin incredible stories.

Kinney thought of him as a ruthless spider spinning nightmares and demons, saints and hellfire. Alma listened raptly, transported as Kostic spoke. Kinney suspected Rose had learned language and a sense of wrong from right from listening to Kostic. His tales always contained a hero; except many of the heroes were from the darkest parts of the underworld.

Alma's understanding of sensuality and gender roles seemed to come from, for lack of a better word, her mothers. Liliana, a hysteric, suffered from bouts of epilepsy. She was considered feeble-minded, yet she had a way about her, an inviting gentleness of spirit. Her long curly hair fell to her back and surrounded her face in shadow, yet a calmness flowed from her. She seemed to feel deep empathy for the others. When Alma was troubled, Liliana soothed her. When the others fought or suffered an episode, Liliana stepped in and softly talked them down, or placed herself fearlessly between them and Alma.

Lynnie Grant, a lifetime ward of the asylum, in her seventies, was as withered as a dead tulip stalk. The years had bent her back into a sharp hook. When she walked, she faced her own stomach. She could not straighten, but would twist her head up to see. Notoriously promiscuous, even at this age, her base and dirty language made the staff lock her in a private ward to keep her from infecting the other inmates. If witches existed, surely Lynnie Grant was one of them.

Kinney could not discern her role in Alma's life and did not care to ponder how Alma could be such a knowledgeable lover. Surely it was not from instruction but Alma's unending passion for Kinney specifically.

Kinney watched and waited and listened to how the inmates related not to Alma but to each other. Every morning when he crawled out of the Tunnels, he wrote copious notes so he would not forget. He would use the information to cut out another cancerous growth of Alma's past, replace it with a wholesome set of memories, and transform her personality into Rose. In this way, he could finally possess his one true love with no shame and no regret.

This morning, she slept. Kinney smiled to himself. He would not have to wait much longer. He had almost everything he needed. He would begin the cleaving soon.

TWENTY-FIVE

"Mallie, I'd like you to assist me with a few things," Kinney said.

She stood in the doorway to his office and looked behind her as if to see if anyone watched.

"It's perfectly above board," Kinney said. "You have nothing to fear from me. Please come in and shut the door."

"It's just that . . . if you forgive sir, there have been doctors, sir, who . . ." she fumbled with her apron, twisted it with her fingers.

"I'm aware of the rumors. Do not fear. I have nothing but a professional interest in you. In fact, I have a proposition for you."

Mallie allowed his statement to register. She entered the office and shut the door. She stayed close to it, her hand poised on the doorknob.

"You have a proposition, sir?" Her cheeks flushed like two bright cherries.

"Tell me, has your family been struck by the wave of job losses?" Kinney knew the answer to this. Most of the country was under a serious economic crisis. The asylum filled with the deranged, which family members could no longer support. Mallie Lyn Peters lived with her single mother and four siblings and her mother mended patients' uniforms. Harvey Briggart had brought great stacks of uniforms for her to fix. Kinney was also aware that she'd lost quite a bit of work lately because Kinney had quietly seen to it to find another seamstress.

Mallie Lyn's face flushed red, and she nodded. "Yes," she said.

"I have a special job for you," Kinney said. "One you will be well compensated for. One that will require some additional time from you on your day off, and perhaps at night. You will be safe, I assure you. I have no interest in you of a physical nature. I simply need a nurse to help me at my new house."

"Your new house, sir?" She looked up at him.

"I have purchased a home not far from here, on the shore of the bay. I have, of course, decided to keep my appointment here at the asylum. You will assist me with some . . ." Kinney paused here as he searched for the word, ". . . experiments if you will. A new method in healing the sick. We will start with one patient."

"One, sir?" Mallie asked softly.

"Just one. And Mallie, if you assist me, perhaps I can send some more work to your mother and your young siblings." He saw her eyes flash, and he could not be certain if it were from gratefulness or if she guessed how much of her family's fate he held in his palms.

"Of course, sir. Whatever you need, sir." She curtsied. "Just a question, sir. Who is the patient?"

Kinney walked to the window to hide his grin. "Alma," he said. "But from now on, we will call her Patient Rose."

Mallie's reaction was not what he'd expected. Instead of fighting him, she said in a strong voice, "Oh, yes, Doctor Kinney. I would be happy to take Alma away from here. To take . . . Rose. And watch over her, I mean, and help you with whatever experiments you need. No one need know. She doesn't really belong here anyway."

When Kinney turned to her, he did not hide his grin. It seemed Mallie Lynne and he had a perfect understanding. "We will begin at once," he said. "I am moving my things to the house tonight."

"Tonight, sir," she said, and she smiled at him in return.

TWENTY-SIX

Rose Kinney was trapped. She could not escape. Her foot had crashed through the top of an old covered well. "Elly!" she cried. "You've got to help me! Get Mama and Papa!"

He reached for her. "I can help you, Rose." He examined her foot; saw the blood around the thin ankle. It reminded him of the pets he'd "operated" on when he was a boy. A large sliver had pierced through her skin. She cried silently, and little Elliott wanted to help her.

"If we get Mama or Papa, you know what they will do. They will be so angry. I can help you. We just have to pull out the sliver, okay?"

Elliott was just seven-years-old when he rescued his sister. He broke off the rotten pieces around her foot. The blood turned her stocking and shoe a deep red. She reached

113

for him, and he half-pulled and half-dragged her free of the well. He quickly undid the ties of her shoe to expose the top of the sliver that was more of a shard of wood.

"It hurts!" she cried. "It's killing me, Elly."

"Don't be silly, Rose. It's only a piece of wood. I'll take it out, and you'll be fine. We won't tell Mama and Papa where we've been. They don't ever need to know. Look at me now, Rose. Just look into my eyes, and when I count to three, I'll . . ." She screamed as he suddenly plucked the shard from her foot. It pulsed with red.

She smiled at him. "We won't tell them?"

"Not in a hundred years," he said solemnly.

"It will be our secret?" He nodded. She kissed him on the lips, quickly.

It was their first of many, many secrets, and perhaps the sweetest of them all.

*

Kinney awoke to Alma stretched lazy as a cat next to him. He traced the curve of her leg, down to the tender arch of her foot. She would need a scar here. A small and tender thing, but it would be the first of her memories.

She stirred.

"Rose," he whispered. "Sweet Rose. I want to take you away from here. Will you come with me?"

"There's no need," she said. "We're happy here, aren't we?"

"But there's a whole world outside these walls. Don't you want to see them?"

She turned to face him, the moonlight sending a shaft of light over her breasts. "I am happy here, Elliot."

"Call me Elly," he said and kissed the tip of her nose.

"Elly."

"Do you love me?" he asked and waited for her to answer. His whole life and purpose seemed to teeter in the silence.

"Yes." she said at last.

"And would you do anything for me?" he asked.

"Anything at all."

"Then you will come with me. We'll leave this place. I can give you a normal life, Rose. Don't you want to be normal?"

She laughed then, a soft laugh, a flutter of moth wings. "This is my normal, and I am happy, my love. But if you want me to make you happy too, then I will go with you."

It was all the promise he needed. He'd take her away from the walls of the asylum and build a different kind of asylum around her, one in which he could take full control of her mind, and delight in the beautiful curves of the body that so reminded him of Rose. He traced the place on her foot where the scar should be; the place where it would be soon.

He wanted everything to be perfect, and it was almost time to make his dreams come true.

TWENTY-SEVEN

With tears and laughter she told us she was leaving, that she was starting a normal life, the kind of life we always envisioned for her. We did not respond. We knew what waited for her outside the walls. There was darkness there and pain and evil. Inside, here, at the asylum, we could protect her and watch over her. Do not go! we wanted to cry, but we bit our tongues and held our silence, as deep as the albino's. We choked on our tears. We hugged her. We allowed.

She was our child, our little bird, and we could no more control her than you can control the clouds.

But we could still watch over her.

Kostic's muscles rippled. Lynnie Grant watched from the shadows. Liliana plotted. Beeler covered the walls with pictures of things to come. We prepared. We waited. We planned.

Alma would need us, and we would be ready.

Fighting with the Devil is not a fair game. We bided our time, ready to fight for her when we were needed most, but first . . . first, we had to let her go. She slipped from our fingers, and we watched her float away, the way a soul leaves its corporeal self and slips away into the ever-lasting night.

Morning would come, and we would be ready. And we would have others waiting with us. We watched from the windows. From the shadows. The bars might keep us from her for a while, but even iron disintegrates if touched with acid.

We stuck out our tongues, and we licked.

TWENTY-EIGHT

Bill Pepperidge pulled his truck up to Building 50 just as Kinney had asked, at precisely 9:00PM. To Bill, 9:00PM was a strange time to make a move, and in December no less, when the nighttime wind had a real bite to it. If Bill had a place to move into, he'd wait until spring to do it. Of course, if Bill had a place like the doctor, maybe he'd make the move right away too. He looked around, noted Kinney standing in front of the door, an air of unrest to him though he stood still. Bill nodded to himself. So much darkness and only more darkness to come.

"Seems you've collected some things there, doctor," Bill said. "I remember just a few months ago driving you up here, and you had naught but one bag with you then. How'd you manage to get all this?" He motioned to the stacks of bags behind him, luggage and what not.

"I've ordered some things for the new house," Kinney said in a way that seemed to end the discussion. Pepperidge tugged on his hat, nodded, and lifted the rest of the bags into the back of his truck. The bed sighed with the weight, just the way the Bill's own bones sighed. He'd worked too hard and too long, with no end in sight. Not with all the folks out of work and the dust bowl happening in the Southwest. If there was one thing Bill knew, it was that as a hired hand there were times where it served you to remain quiet and stupid.

He didn't look at the woman, or he tried not to. The little Irish girl had brought her out, wrapped her in a big blanket. The young woman was beautiful and clearly terrified out of her skin. She looked around as if she'd never seen a night sky. Of course, if she was a loony (and she certainly looked like a loony) maybe everything was always new to her. Sometimes the mind was broken that way. Bill took this in without appearing to notice a thing. He'd worked at the asylum a long time. There were certain skills a man developed over time.

He didn't even acknowledge her presence as Kinney pried her free from the Irish girl's embrace. He took the frightened woman by the elbow guided her into the truck. She seemed to not know what to do. Not how to get up into it or what to expect. Kinney had to lift her into the truck, and when he took the seat next to her, she seemed to try to crawl inside Kinney's own body. He held her.

Bill climbed in to. Didn't have to worry about touching her, as she sat so close to the doctor. "We ready?"

Bill asked and the doctor nodded his head. The woman almost jumped out of her dress at the sound of the engine coming to, but Bill knew better than to ask.

Truth be told, other doctors had taken lovers just as it appeared Kinney was doing. There was a fair share of loose women in the asylum, Bill knew, and sometimes they ended up as housemaids at cottages for a time. And sometimes they weren't heard of ever again. It didn't matter to Bill. It seemed the women went willingly enough. Shoot, some of the women were so feeble minded they didn't know up from down. Maybe staying with one of the doctors gave them a little bit more comfort for a time. What mattered to Bill was that he'd have money to put food on the table for his wife and four kids and grandchild. Sometimes, you just had to close your eyes to things.

It took a lot for Bill to drive to the doctor's new residence in silence, but he did it. And was rewarded handsomely for it.

TWENTY-NINE

To Alma, the outside world filled with scents and sounds she did not understand. There were no walls to keep her secure, no loving family to hold her. She tried to press close to Doctor Kinney, but she felt no warmth. She wanted her papas, her mammas. The world breathed ice on her face, and it hurt. She wanted the shadows of her underground, not the great dark ceiling above her. She wanted her woodland creatures and her music and her box of special things. She did not understand what was happening or how they were sitting and moving so fast. The world was so loud, and she pressed her hands to her ears to drown out the sound, but still it seeped in. She began to cry. It started in the depths of her stomach, where her deepest pain resided. The tears and anger formed, and she let it pour out.

121

The Doctor held her. "Hussshhhh," he said. Just that. "Hussshhh." And Alma stilled. It was a magic word, a word that meant be quiet or they will find you. It was a word from her childhood and her growing years. It was a word almost as close as the name she had chosen for herself. Hussshhh. She closed her eyes. She let herself be rocked to and fro, the way Mama Liliana would hold her and sing to her.

After a time, the sounds and motion stopped. Kinney took her hand and helped her reach the ground. "This is your home, Rose," he said to her.

Alma looked around. She knew that Kinney called her "Rose" and sometimes she answered to it. It was so dark out that the world now seemed smaller, and that was a comfort.

"Say, thank you, dear Kinney." His voice was a needle.

Alma closed her eyes. Her family had warned her of this moment, when she would be discovered and taken from them. She knew this could happen. She also knew though she felt alone, she was not. They had taught her many things, ways to defend herself, weapons to use in case of danger. She would be able to use all their warnings and protect herself.

The first weapon was to make them believe you. Make them believe you would give them what they wanted. Alma could do that. She was a very talented girl.

"Thank you, dear Kinney," Alma said evenly. She smiled at him.

The second weapon was to remember everything they did to you. Remember. Remember. Remember. Alma's eyes were open now. Very wide open, indeed.

Kinney led her into the house and out of the darkness. Alma continued to smile even as the light in the house blinded her.

THIRTY

December 18, 1933

To

Mrs. Johnson, Housekeeper

Mallie Lyn Peters, Attending Nurse

Eleanor Koepp, Tutor

Rose's schedule is to be followed every day, consistently, for the next three months. Routine will help eradicate her previous experiences. In routine, she will find comfort and freedom. Miss Peters will attend to Rose when she is available; all other times Mrs. Johnson will see that she stays on schedule. Miss Koepp will maintain charge during her scheduled times. She is to keep to her own room at all other times. Excursions into town are allowed with written permission.

5:30AM Rise from bed and ablutions

6:00AM Breakfast of porridge, meat, various fruit

7:00AM Morning walk

7:30AM Tutor arrives for lessons in literature, basic mathematics, housekeeping, cooking, manners

11:00AM Lunch with tutor

12:00PM Afternoon walk

12:30PM Afternoon memory exercises. Use repetition of provided memories to replace those of her childhood. Begin with page 1, early childhood, and do not move forward until I deem necessary.

4:00PM Rest. Time may be filled with needlework, painting, gardening and other calming activities.

6:00PM I shall return from the asylum and will join Rose for dinner. She is to wear one of her three finest dresses.

7:00PM Memory exercises with me begin promptly. Do not disturb us.

10:00PM Bedtime.

–Doctor Elliott Kinney–

THIRTY-ONE

Kinney's new life glowed. It virtually glowed! He found such excitement in his work now that he had a home and purpose again. At the asylum, there was a softness about him, and his endless coughing and colds had subsided. He was less apt to prescribe hydrotherapy for misbehaving patients and more willing to give them a second chance. He talked at the dinner table with his colleagues and the Board on the nights he was required to stay. All other times he flew through his day and followed his checklist. He saw patients, he prescribed, he monitored, and he read the most recent research.

At night, Bill Pepperidge drove him the short distance to his new home, a lovely home surrounded by woods and on a hill overlooking the bay. With every moment Kinney drew closer to his home, his heart beat a little bit faster. He did not fully breathe until they pulled up to the house with the dining room illuminated from within. He had to stop himself from running up the stairs because he knew she waited for him.

He liked her best in the red dress. A red dress for his dear Rose.

Before entering the dining room, he took a calming breath, gathered his wits, and turned the doorknob. There she was, waiting. Candles lit, their meal prepared for them, she looked so beautiful with her waves of shadow dark hair. She turned to him and smiled and said the words he'd practiced with her. At first, the words had sounded hollow and unfeeling, but with continued repetition took on new meaning. It was so simple, really! You could give anyone a new memory if you simply repeated it long enough . . . and tonight . . . tonight . . . she said the words for the first time.

"Hello, husband. Welcome home."

Kinney stopped and stared at her. A dark curl had fallen across her eye. She looked at him, her smile firmly in place. Firm. Cold. He reached for her, pressed his lips to hers.

"Hello, Rose," he said. "Very well done. Next time, kiss me back."

Rose nodded. He patted her shoulder then moved to sit across from her. They would eat dinner in silence, as she did not have the skills yet to carry on the type of conversation he might have had with his first Rose. Through repetition, she would finally get it right, and then, and then . . . well. He smiled to himself and reached for the roasted pork. They would begin practicing the next phase tonight. First, he would teach her how to kiss him back, then all the right things she should say.

He thinly sliced the pork and placed a piece on Rose's plate. There was no noise save their silverware scraping on the china.

THIRTY-TWO

Mallie Lyn Peters watched from the kitchen door, cracked open. A sliver of light fell across her eye, but from a distance she would be invisible. Kinney paid her no mind, any way. He was too focused on his dinner with Alma.

Mallie's new life was a curious existence. She worked at the asylum during the day and things ran as normal. She rarely saw Charlie, as with Alma gone, there was no more need to meet each other in the tunnels. She missed him, but she did not miss the way he eyed Alma. That morning, though, she'd run to the kitchen where he loaded in wood, and she'd given him a jar of preserves.

"Why, thank you, Mallie . . . " he'd said, and quickly added, "Miss Peters."

"It's my pleasure, Mr. Young. I made them myself I did. From spring rhubarb," she'd returned, blushing to her toes. She replayed that conversation over and over.

Months ago she would've gone home to her mother and siblings after her work at the asylum. Now she had a room of her own in this expansive house with Doctor Kinney and Alma. Rose. She wasn't sure what he wanted to call her (or why) and so mostly she avoided using her name at all.

In her work at the asylum, Mallie had been witness to, and an accomplice, in many of the therapies given. She'd strapped patients down while they were administered remedies. She'd seen seizures that rattled brains. Once, an inmate had bitten off her own tongue in an effort to remain silent. Horrible things. And the therapies never really seemed to help. Mallie secretly believed many of the patients were beyond help. It wasn't just the feeble-minded ones, the ones with apparent physical deformities. There were others with fractured souls, and a few who possessed no soul at all. Mallie wasn't sure if Alma could be healed, because she hadn't yet figured out what was wrong with her. So Mallie watched and observed as she had done at the asylum.

Kinney moved to sit next to Alma. "Rose," he said. When Alma did not look up at him, he said her name again, but this time there was an edge to his voice. "Rose!"

She looked at him. Mallie could not see her expression, but she felt anger pouring off the girl.

"I want to tell you a story about how we met."

"We met at my home," Alma said. "I came to you one night, and I took you."

"No. You did not. That's a dream, Rose. A dream. We met on the shores of Lake Michigan, in Grand Haven. We were both vacationing with our families at the same resort. You stood in the water, your dress lifted to your knees. And do you remember what happened next?"

She did not answer.

"There was a great undertow, and when the waves crashed in, you lost your footing and . . . "

"I fell?" Alma asked softly.

Kinney nodded, apparently pleased. "You fell. I was walking by at that moment and I ran into the water to rescue you."

"You rescued me. I fell in the water."

"It was cold. Freezing. I carried you out of the water and you were . . . "

"Shivering."

Kinney nodded again. "Shivering. And you said . . . "

"It's like the lake wanted me to swallow me whole."

"And I said, you must take more care. And you looked at me, Rose, you looked at me and said . . . "

"If I had taken care, I wouldn't be in your arms right now. I rather like being in your arms right now." Alma looked directly at Kinney. A light illuminated her beauty. "I'm Rose," she said to the doctor.

Kinney nodded, and Mallie wondered if his expression was one of pleasure.

"And I am Elliott Kinney," he said, and shook Rose's hand.

Mallie would think of her as Rose now. She could see this was what the doctor wanted. He wanted everyone to believe she was someone else.

Mallie drew away from the kitchen door and let it close silently. She'd seen them rehearse this scene over and over. What was the point? Could Alma actually believe this was her memory? She seemed to. But why? What kind of healing could false thoughts do for a person?

She did not want to think about it. She did not want to question what was going on in this house or about to go on in this house. She wanted her pay and to help her family, and she wanted, most of all, she wanted Charlie Young to herself.

THIRTY-THREE

Alma was empty. Empty. In her room at night in the doctor's house, she could close her eyes and be in the comforting shadows of her childhood home. She missed the pictures papa Tim had drawn for her. She wanted papa Robert to come to her and practice swordplay. She wanted mamas Liliana and Lynnie to sing her to sleep. This time though, when she called for them, they did not come. No one came, save the doctor. She stopped calling.

She missed the sound of water dripping in the tunnels. Missed running her hands across the surface of the brick. Missed running as fast as she could through the curving underground passage. She knew it so well she could run with her eyes closed with no fear of tripping. And when the asylum slept, she explored. She played. And as she grew older, she *tended*.

She was, contrary to what Kinney suspected, not at all a blank slate. She knew of the world, and she knew where her family slept at night. She knew they had trouble in The Outside World and had come to the Asylum because they could not live anywhere else. She knew not to mention potatoes to papa Robert. She knew to never approach mama Liliana from behind. She knew that her family was different and she did not care. She did not yearn for anything other than what she had. What needs did she have? She had a loving home and adventures. As she grew older, Liliana and mama Lynnie explained to her the peculiar hunger that grew within her and how she could quiet it down by using a man.

Kinney was not her first lover. She'd taken them before, in the darkest of nights, sometimes only once, sometimes repeatedly. They thought of her as a ghost or a hallucination. She liked it that way. With Kinney, though, she had felt something different. He looked at her differently than the others. There was a hint of fierceness in his wanting of her. If only Alma had figured it out earlier the way she had with the other inmates of the asylum.

Growing up within its walls, at night she had explored the belly of the hospital . . . and over time, she had grown to know the inmates. She could sneak into their wards at night. She told stories. She danced. She sang. And they loved her. She never feared for her safety because her family watched out for her. Before approaching an inmate, Alma studied them. She watched them. She could feel how they were broken, and as one would avoid touching a wound when trying to heal it, Alma avoided those broken parts of their spirits. You could read a person's emotions from the words their body spoke. How the body tensed or relaxed, how a face contracted or pinched, how eyes flashed at you with humor or menace. Alma had a talent to calm and connect. To heal. After their treatments, Alma would go to them, touch their foreheads, and they looked up at her and found comfort.

Her one mistake was that she had not taken enough time to observe Kinney. She had wanted that peculiar closeness with him, to take pleasure from him, and she had taken him wildly. But she should have noted that flash in his eyes.

Like everyone else at the asylum, Kinney was broken, and he was the first person whom Alma had met where she could not figure out which wounds to avoid in order to heal him.

In her new room and new life, she waited. She closed her eyes. She sang softly to herself and dreamed of running in the tunnels. For now, she would give Kinney everything he wanted. She would control the language of her body. But when she finally figured out the cracks in his spirit, when she knew the answer to what ailed him, then, and only then would she take action.

She was happy here for a time, but had no doubt that she would return to her family. She served a greater purpose at the asylum. She was their secret, their dark angel, and she loved them with all her might.

THIRTY-FOUR

Kinney dreamed of walking on the beach of Grand Haven with his Rose, his first Rose. She ran ahead of him, laughing, a laugh of pure hysteria.

"You can't catch me!" she called to him.

He ran. It was November and the lake had not cooled enough yet. By January, entire waves would be frozen mid-crash, but now, the water was simply as cool as ice but still a liquid. Rose ran, her dress pressing against her body. It began to drizzle. Kinney felt his lungs expand and his heart beat. He had to catch her! He had to.

And then he did. She turned to look at him and her bare foot caught. She did not fall as much as fly, landing face down in the sand.

"You are a foolish, foolish girl," he said.

She turned to face him but did not get up. A button had been lost from the top of her dress, and her breasts heaved against the cloth that restrained them. Sand clung to her neck. "I am no girl," she spat back at him.

"Stand up! Stand up at once!"

She refused again. He did not think, but reacted, allowing his hand to fly through the cool air and smack her with such force that electricity jolted through him. She stopped laughing at once.

"Do it again," she said.

He did. Then something strange happened to Kinney. A deep, residing anger uncoiled within him and he hit her, shook her, pushing her harder into the ground. She heaved and bucked against him, and the animal that had been sleeping inside of him rose. He clawed at her dress, tugged it up, and all the while she laughed, begging him . . . do it . . . do it . . . he pushed himself between her legs and then, oh, great release . . . great beauty to be where he had always wanted to be, so warm, so wet, so very, very wrong . . .

It was over in moments.

He pulled back, tucked himself away and looked at his hands that were not his, looked around the beach to see if anyone had witnessed his monstrous act.

"Who's the crazy one now?" Rose asked him. "It isn't me, Elliott. It's you. It's you! You! You! You!"

He longed to throw her into the water, and hold her head beneath cool surface. Instead, he got to his feet and walked away, leaving her in the sand, an abandoned doll.

Kinney woke with a start. He was in her room—in Rose's room. His new Rose. She slept beside, him breathing heavily. His fingers tingled with electricity again, and the familiar sleeping anger within him began to roil.

Things were not moving fast enough. He needed more time with her. If he did more memory exercises, more actively tried to wash her mind free of her own history, he would have his Rose back to him, only this time she would be perfect. He thought of the things he hadn't tried: more aggressive therapies, hypnosis, reshaping her personality through discipline. There was so much to do. So much to do! First, he would put in a leave of absence at the asylum. He would devote all his time to creating the perfect wife, one who would not laugh at him or taunt him, and one who was not of his same blood.

Kinney reached for her bare shoulder and drew his fingers across her skin.

Suddenly, he realized the episode on the beach with Rose hadn't been a dream at all, but a memory.

THIRTY-FIVE

In the halls of the asylum, a storm brewed. It began with a whisper: *"Kinney took Alma"* and was repeated and repeated until the syllables slurred. The words drifted through the staff at Building 50, the three floors of the women's ward, and finally slithered under the locked doors of the men's ward, pouncing on Robert Kostic's chest. He twisted in bed, writhing as if attacked by tiny knives.

Alma was gone.

Cut.

Kinney had taken her.

Slice.

Kinney was not coming back.

Stab.

Kostic bolted awake.

Though the drugs of his 'therapy' pulled at him, he shook his head as if he could shake free of their grasp. Whatever it took, whatever face he needed to put on to convince the foolish doctors that he was normal, he would wear. What was normal anyway? Find out how a doctor understood normal, and be that for them. Change for another doctor.

Kostic silently stepped out of bed, touching the cold floor with his bare feet. Solitary would last a few more days. Though he couldn't actually hear the men in the ward breathing in their sleep, he felt the rise and fall of their lungs. He bent to the floor, placed his hands flat against it, and pushed. He would do pushups until his muscles bulged and burned. And then he would run in place. And then he would box. He would be ready for what was coming.

He sent a whisper back through the corridor, knowing the words would eventually find Kinney: *I'm coming for you.*

The words took flight and raced ahead of him into the darkness.

PART FOUR – Home

Dear Dr. Kinney:

The Board of the Northern Michigan Insane Asylum accepts your request for personal time off. The transition from physician in a hospital for the body to an institution devoted to illnesses of the mind is a difficult one. We have reviewed your log sheets and have discovered that for the past few months you have worked approximately sixty hours a week, an exhausting load for any professional. We have agreed to grant you the holidays off with pay. You are asked to return to the Asylum on February 1, 1933. At that time, we hope you will resume your duties to the patients who have come to rely on you.

December 17, 1932

. . . According to the State of Michigan Health Department, the rate of new tuberculosis cases is on the rise. While not officially an epidemic, the disease is spreading at an alarming rate. The Northern Michigan Insane Asylum has donated one of the wings of the institution to offset Munson Hospital's overburdened facility. If you or a loved one develops symptoms common to tuberculosis, like excessive coughing or blood coming from your mouth, please seek medical treatment at the asylum at once. It is a closed ward and will allow you to fully recuperate and lessen the chances of spreading the disease.

–From the Record Eagle

THIRTY-SIX

Alma placed her hand over the curve of her abdomen. She could no longer fit into the dresses her husband had given her. For Kinney called himself her husband, and she thought of him as such. She thought she could remember their wedding on the shore of Lake Superior.

No . . . Michigan. Lake Michigan. And the wind was warm, and the waves were gentle and the sun shone as if blessing them with good fortune. She remembered . . . cold walls . . . no . . . cold . . .

"Waves," Kinney had whispered into her ear.

"Waves," she repeated, held firmly in his trance. He'd whispered memories into her ear over and over, painted pictures so vivid she began to dream them and feel they were real. Weren't they real? Real was what you could touch and feel and hold and taste, but wasn't it also memory? You

144

couldn't touch or hold or taste a memory, but it was real.
Wasn't it?

She remembered walking down the beach hand in
hand with her husband. She'd held a parasol, and the waves
surprised them by splashing up and covering their feet. The
water was so shocking that she let go of the parasol and sent
it tumbling in the air. Kinney chased it right into the water,
captured it, and brought it back to her. They laughed at his
wet clothes, at how he shivered, and she had never felt such
love.

He called her "Rose" over and over, and that was who
she was. But she was also someone else. She was . . . warm
hands and faces around her, picking her up when she fell,
passing from arm to arm, stories told, math, art, dancing with
women at night, learning to read pain and see horror spread
across someone's face, talking to their clear center to bring
them back to her. Back to her.

She needed to come back to herself.

Something was not right.

Again she traced her stomach. There was something
not right with her mind and her memories, and now
something most assuredly not right with her stomach. Alma
(Rose) sat in a chair and breathed heavily. She could no
longer inhale and make her stomach flat. It would not flatten.
She wasn't sure what was happening to her, but felt perhaps it
was like the stories her . . . who? Who told her? She vaguely
remembered hearing her papa tell her about demons and the
fight against evil, and the other papa drawing pictures on her

walls. But that wasn't right. It couldn't be right. A girl didn't have two papas. She had one. And her father's name was Edward and her mother's name was . . . Lucy . . . and her name was Rose.

At that moment something fluttered in her stomach, and she became aware of the creature inside her.

THIRTY-SEVEN

Mallie Lyn Peters was in the kitchen when she heard Mrs. Kinney screaming. She thought of her now as Mrs. Kinney as it was so much easier than Rose or Alma or whomever the doctor wanted to believe she was. The Doctor insisted they had married, though no one saw the actual ceremony. There was a wedding dress in the attic, but it seemed like it would have been too long for her.

No. Mallie Lyn knew what was going on, but had little power to stop it. Her welfare was at stake. Worse than that, the welfare of her family. If she weren't helping the missus, someone else would. "I don't know that I agree with his experiments," she'd thought to herself over and over, "but there's nothing I can do." At the same time, they didn't seem to do harm exactly. It's just that the woman who he claimed as his wife had started out so wild and raw and beautiful in a way. Now, she was like so many of the doctors' wives: pale and timid and as tremulous as a butterfly. This wouldn't happen to her, Mallie assured herself. When Charlie finally asked her to marry him, and he would, she wouldn't lose an ounce of who she was to him. Not one ounce.

She abandoned these thoughts along with the slice of cake she ate and ran up the long stairs to attend to the mistress.

"Madam! Madam Kinney? Are you all right in there? May I come in, ma'am?" Mallie hesitated at the door. There was a lock on the door, but it was there to lock Mrs. Kinney *in*, not keep others out. Mallie didn't want to barge in and upset the doctor if he found out. She placed her ear to the door and confirmed that her Mistress inside was crying. Mallie opened the door and gently shut it behind her.

Mrs. Kinney stood in front of her, naked, and achingly beautiful. Her long, dark hair fell over her shoulders and touched the top of her heavy breasts. Mallie noted at once the curve of the woman's abdomen.

"What is wrong with me?" Mrs. Kinney asked in a shaking voice. "There's a creature . . . "

"A creature?" A deep sadness penetrated Mallie's heart. She'd really thought Mrs. Kinney had recovered and had managed to avoid the illnesses that floated in the asylum like a mist.

"A creature! Here!" Mrs. Kinney pointed to her stomach.

It took Mallie a moment to understand.

"Why . . . Ma'am, don't you know? That's not a creature, but a child. You've got an angel growing inside you, you do." Mallie smiled warmly at the woman and reached for her robe. She draped it tenderly across the woman's shoulders. She seemed to flinch at the touch then relaxed into the comfort of the robe. "Ma'am, sit down. Please. I'll get you something to eat. You've got to eat more when you're eating for two."

Mrs. Kinney sat on the side of her bed. She did not acknowledge Mallie, but turned instead to look out the window.

"A child," she said as Mallie left the room. Mallie wasn't sure if she'd said the word with hope or fear.

Outside it was swirling white: a blizzard.

THIRTY-EIGHT

Inside the asylum, chaos swirled. White sheets flapped as orderlies made beds, moved equipment, set up screens between the beds, then abandoned doing so when they ran out of both. The coughing could be heard even outside the ward. At first men and women were separated, but within a week the ward filled with both sexes. They came into our space and pushed us out, then we caught their coughing, too.

They lay in our beds at first, and then on cots, in chairs, and when there were no more chairs, they huddled on the floor. Pretty soon, we stopped knowing where they started and we began. The coughing became a chorus of sprinkled blood. Fevers spiked, and nurses ran from bed to bed tending the sick. There was running. Cries of pain. Screams of pleading to be released. The Superintendent stood at the entrance to the ward, watching the chaos rise and crash like waves.

We listened. We were part of the chaos and the illness and the shadows . . .

"You are here for your own good!" called Dr. Christopher Grooms. "For the value of society! You are here to heal!"

To that, a frail woman with stringy blond hair said: "We are here to die!"

"I don't know what to do," the head nurse said to him. "We don't have any more beds left, sir. We don't have the staff to support this. Tell the city we cannot . . ."

Mr. Grooms stopped her with a glance. "You have no concept at all with what we're dealing with. The state has offered us money, real money and . . ." He breathed heavily. "Take over Ward C. Combine the three levels of asylum patients into one area except for the highest paying ones. Let them continue to have their space until we can figure something out for them. Call in all support staff and physicians who are on vacation. We will ride this out. It's only an epidemic. Epidemics pass . . ." He did not finish the sentence, but the nurse understood. Epidemics passed when everyone died.

We knew this, too. We waited. We held our breath, but some of us coughed.

When the rooms began to burst and the coughing became a storm, we met in the Tunnels to discuss our Alma.

"Is she all right?"

"Why hasn't she contacted us?"

"You said she would have her fill of him and come back to us. Why hasn't she come back to us?"

Tim, the mute albino, drew on a pad of paper. It was a sketch of Mallie Lynn Peters, and we knew what he meant. That she would know. That she would tell us.

We found her talking to Charlie Young, her creamy skin flecked with pink, not from coughing but from want. She tried to hide it, but we knew, as did Charlie Young. A few looks and batted eyes, and Mallie Lynn curtsied and met us in the shadows of the asylum.

She whispered to us, her voice a steady thrum, and we felt her fear in our bones. "He's doing something to her mind," she said. "And now she's with child, too. At first, she asked to see you all, and now she's talking about two other people as if they're her parents. It's as if . . . " she crossed herself. "It's as if he's trying to take away all that she is and replace it with someone else. He has me do her hair like this old photograph. A photograph of his sister and it's just not natural."

Kostic heaved a heavy breath. We pulled him back so he would not hurt the girl. She was but a butterfly, and he'd crush her if he weren't careful. Through clenched teeth he said the words we all wanted to say: "But is she okay?"

Mallie looked at us, and we saw the tears in her eyes. "If you're asking me does she belong in this place like the others, then, no sir. She does not. She is well. But if you're asking me if she's safe outside these walls, then again, no sir, she is not. She is in great danger, and I fear for the babe she's carrying."

We heard footsteps, and Mallie ran off to help with other patients. It was enough. We'd heard enough.

"You know what we must do," we whispered. Our four bodies became one. We drew strength. We planned.

And when the epidemic above reached its height, an inmate disappeared from the asylum. Robert Kostic was no longer in solitary. No longer in the Men's Ward. The orderlies assumed he'd been sent to the TB ward, and the TB ward no longer cared who entered. They only recorded how many they were treating to secure funds from the state. Kostic slipped quietly out of the asylum and straight into the brewing storm.

THIRTY-NINE

Alma stood at the window; her dress lay out on the bed. It turned her stomach looking at it, the way her nights with Kinney now did. In the beginning, he had been interesting to her. A curiosity. She had learned from her mothers on how to take pleasure from a man. At first, she'd been so hungry for him, but then she'd grown tired. Tired of his games, of his silly experiments, of this outside world of light and candles and dressing up. She'd thought at first it would be like walking into one of the paintings Papa Tim drew for her. The beautiful illustrations where lovely women were adored and cherished.

This place was no fairy tale.

And Doctor Kinney was madder than anyone at the asylum. She could see it in his eyes–that flash of darkness. Of evil. She'd had enough of him, and now it was time to go.

154

She'd taken pleasure from him and the seed of a new life, and now she was finished.

Yet . . . how? How did she leave? Would he stop her? Hurt her? Kill her?

Her parents had warned her of the *Dark Madness.* Of madness that could not be reasoned with or talked down or soothed, the way she did the others. This kind of evil was rare but very real. She could envision Kinney reaching his claws around her throat. If she told him she was leaving–would he try to snuff out her breath? Her answer came from within. YES.

She would stay then. She would stay until she could safely escape, and she would figure out how to stop Kinney from coming after her or her family.

As she made her decision, a white hand reach out to her from the swirl of white and pressed against the glass. For a moment she could not breathe, then she smiled, and placed her smaller palm against his.

FORTY

Outside was a blur of white. Kinney stood at the window of his large home and watched the wind whip the snow into giant drifts. The snow fell in a heavy sheet, covering rocks and benches, deck chairs, the wheelbarrow and eventually Kinney's car. The world was swallowed whole. He returned to the fireplace, a smile spreading coolly across his face. With most of the staff, save Mallie Lyn Peters, away for the holiday, Kinney had his Rose all to himself, and no one would be able to interrupt them.

He sat in his favorite green velvet chair and listened to the fire crackle. Rose was upstairs dressing. He'd given her a very special outfit to wear for this evening, one he'd had recreated from photographs. The one Rose—the first Rose— had been wearing when she'd . . .

The fire popped, startling Kinney. He no longer wanted to think of the first Rose and the new Rose. He wanted one Rose. One Rose who would be his wife and not his sister. One Rose who breathed and was warm with life, not cold and worm-eaten, and he wanted her to be perfect. Tonight, his wife would wear the dress she'd worn when she'd almost died. Almost. Yes! Almost! Because his wife had not died at all! He hadn't chased her into the frigid water and held her under until she stopped fighting him. He hadn't cured her diseased mind with death . . . but with love. Why even now his Rose, fully recuperated and looking more perfect than ever, was dressing for him in a white gown upstairs.

He imagined her stepping into the gown, her bare legs smooth. He could hear the dress being pulled up over her hips, and the image of the white fabric against her smooth skin caused his blood to roil within him. The dress slid over the curves of her hips, over her full breasts. She reached behind her back and tucked the buttons into the loops. Later, Kinney would tear those buttons free, rip the dress from her smooth body, and reclaim all he had lost.

He heard the footsteps running down the hall. She was running to him! Running to him at last! His Rose! His wife!

Mallie cried. It was Mallie, wasn't it, and not his Rose? Kinney stood and turned to watch Mallie run to the stairs, stumble, and roll completely down them, her body tumbling like a sack of laundry.

There was silence in the house, save for the crackling of the fire, and a great gust of wind outside swirling snow ever closer to the windows trapping them inside. Kinney did not run to Mallie immediately. He processed the words she had cried before falling down the stairs: "She's gone, sir! Rose is gone! He's taken her!"

Mallie groaned and reached for Kinney.

He spun on his heels and went to fetch his jacket and gloves. The stupid girl could die there for all he cared. He wanted only one thing: Rose. He had prepared so long for this moment. What was his wife thinking? What was she doing? In trying to recreate his beloved, had he also duplicated her diseased mind?

He knew where she went. Of course. She was a fragile bird. A homing pigeon. There was only one thing for him to do—head to the asylum. He'd thought he could take her away from there, wipe her memory like a chalkboard, and start afresh. She had no idea what happiness lie in front of them and now . . . now . . .

The sleeping beast within Kinney twisted and turned. He took a breath, and for the first time in over three years allowed himself to fully feel the rage that lived within. There was much to be angry for. He loved his sister and could not possess her. He'd once taken her as his own and had never been able to duplicate that delight, not even with his new Rose writhing on top of him.

The anger curled deep and black within him, poised to strike and let out its poison. He had felt it once before and had reached his hands around his sister's throat and squeezed, trying to stop her laughter, and he had stopped her.

Somehow, in all of his planning, he must have gone very, very wrong. If his new Rose ran from him, if she fled back to her old life, he could do only one thing. Eliminate the experiment. Start again. But before he would do that, he would make everyone pay. Everyone. If only they had left him and Rose in peace to live their life quietly. But they hadn't, had they? No. The world was against him. It had always been against him.

Kinney swung open the door and ran into the white. He saw the tire tracks in the snow and knew a way to cut across the grounds and catch them as the road swerved.

It took only moments for him to leave the house and Mallie's cries far behind him.

FORTY-ONE

Alma clung to Kostic in the truck as the old man Pepperidge drove. Kostic breathed through it. He did not like to be touched, but made an exception for Alma. Alma was the exception to everything. He could talk to her. See her. Help her. She was the child he might have had once upon a time. He patted her head. Still, she did not let go.

"Where are we going, Papa?" she asked him. He did not answer because they all knew where they were headed. Home.

The old man Pepperidge spoke to him but kept his eyes on the swirl of white outside. "It's a bad night, Robert," he warned.

"I know it's a bad night, but it's the best night for this." Kostic said. He struggled with the words.

"Why do you want to go back to the asylum? It's foolish. Surely my sister would take you back in again. She loves you."

Robert Kostic clenched his teeth, flexing his muscles as he did. Alma clung ever fiercely to him. He did not like to talk about his mother, nor did he like anyone knowing that the old groundsman was his uncle. Kostic was well enough to know the family kept him a secret, but they didn't know he kept them a secret in return. No one knew about them.

The truck lurched on the road, tires locked.

"Hold on!" Bill said. His thin arms flexed and spun the wheel. Without thinking, Kostic reached over, and with a single hand, wrestled the truck back on the road. The truck swerved, wheels spun, snow swirled. They turned sideways and came to a stop.

"Jesus," Bill muttered. "If that's not a sign you shouldn't go back, I don't know what is."

Robert pointed into the snow. The headlights lit a path in front of them only inches wide, but they could see the dark figure standing in front of them.

Alma began to cry.

"It's not possible," Bill said. "He was back at the house."

Kostic held onto Alma, pulling her close. He knew that not only was it possible, it was predictable. Dr. Elliott Kinney was a demon, and everyone knew demons could fly.

He kissed Alma's forehead. "Take her home," he said to his uncle. Kostic released her, opened the door, and

161

climbed out of the truck, grabbing the baseball bat that had rested at his feet.

"Kostic," Dr. Kinney sneered.

As a form of greeting, Kostic raised the bat and swung.

FORTY-TWO

"What's happening!" Alma cried. She tried to see in front of them, but the old man driving the truck reversed so quickly, the storm swallowed her husband and her papa.

"Don't pay attention to them," the old man said, his voice loud and piercing. "We'll be home soon enough."

Alma tried to stop from shaking. It was too much to bear. Too much! She'd left the only home she'd ever had and moved to that horrible room. She'd loved Kinney as her mothers had instructed her, with her body, but he had wanted to possess all of her. He had tried to make her into something she was not. She was not his wife. She was not Rose. And now a child grew within her, a creature with his brain and soul, and she could not stand it. She could not stand it!

But the child was partially hers. Half of her. So maybe . . . maybe there was hope.

"Stop crying," the old man said. "It's a helluva drive. A horrible storm. I need to think."

She tried to swallow the tears. They wedged in her throat. She closed her eyes. If she closed her eyes, she could pretend none of this was real. She was not on the road in the cold in a storm. She was in her little room with the pictures on the walls and her family around her. She was happy. She was not going to grow a baby. She was a baby herself. She was Alma. Just Alma. And she was loved.

The truck slid to a stop. "We're here," he said.

Alma opened her eyes and smiled. He had taken her home, as he'd said. Building 50 of the asylum loomed in front of them. "Home!" she breathed.

FORTY-THREE

Kostic stepped out of the truck, baseball bat clenched in his hand. He did not breathe or move but stared into the feral eyes of the doctor—the doctor who had held him down and nearly drowned him, who had performed medical 'experiments' on him by pushing him to the brink of death then yanking him back. This doctor who had not really tried to heal him or the voices who spoke to him, but to beat him into submission.

"And what do you plan on doing with that?" Dr. Kinney said.

Kostic cocked his head slightly. The outline of Dr. Kinney shimmered. Kostic blinked and the shimmer fell away, revealing the man as he really was.

Elliot Kinney stood before him, half man and half snake, his eyes deep black slits, his skin a shimmering green. His black tongue flicked out of his mouth.

"You think you have *ssssome* power over me?" Kinney hissed.

Kostic took hold of the anger at the pit of his stomach, raised the bat like a sledgehammer, and charged. He thought about Alma and what the doctor had tried to take from her. He thought about his family at the asylum, his new family, the one he had chosen for himself. The snow swirled around him, and he brought the bat down, aiming for the doctor's head.

Somehow, Kinney stopped him. He lifted his hands, grabbed the bat and stopped it from smashing his own head. Kostic screamed, rage washing over him like liquid fire. He charged, head first, pushing Kinney into a bank of snow. He hit him in the face, again and again, until the serpent doctor's skin parted and fresh drops of red peppered the white.

"Are you even human?" Kostic shouted. He needed no answer. He knew. He reached his hands around the doctor's neck and squeezed. The doctor thrashed beneath him as if being forced underwater, and Kostic smiled.

He knew the doctor clawed at his back, but did not realize until it was too late, that he had reached for a scalpel. He did not realize it until the scalpel plunged into his back again and again, causing Kostic to rear up and backward.

The doctor leapt at him, and Kostic swore he didn't hold a scalpel, but his own fingers had become scalpels, disguised as claws.

"I. Will. Make. You. Pay." The doctor said and slashed at him.

Kostic tried to fend him off. He was stronger than the doctor and fueled by anger born of love for Alma. He delayed him, but soon, after the stabbing and the thrashing to his face, the world turned from white to red, and the doctor succeeded, at last, in bringing poor Kostic to his knees.

The snow swallowed them both.

FORTY-FOUR

"Go on in! Now!" The old man and gave her shoulder a shove. Alma fell from the truck and landed on her knees in the snow. The tires behind her spun, and the truck lurched backward, taking the light with it. Alma slowly got to her feet, careful not to slip on the ice. She felt a flutter in her stomach and wondered if she'd waken the creature now growing within her.

Lights lit Building 50, and Alma drew forward, a moth pulled to its flaming doom. She walked up the steps. Before she got to the door, she could hear the coughing. Alma could run if she wanted, she could turn around and crawl to the safety of her room and never emerge again. She could slip inside the shadows, become one if she wanted, but something within her had changed. She raised her slender hand and knocked.

The doors opened. Alma stared straight into the eyes of a nurse she'd seen a hundred times, but one who had never acknowledged her. She was a ghost to all of them. They'd seen her dancing in the halls and turned their backs. They'd heard her cries in the tunnels and kept on walking. They left bread for her and ribbons but they never called her by name. Now, she stood in front of one, determined to be seen.

The nurse looked like a giant potato. She was so thick she seemed to have lost the appearance of a neck. Alma shivered. The nurse looked her from head to foot and then said in a gruff voice "I know who you are."

Alma nodded.

"Do you think if I put you in one of these dresses that you could give us a hand with the sick? And not say a word to anyone about it? Pretend you're mute or something. But God help me, people are dying, and I need the help. You and me can figure out what you want in return later. Could you do that for me?"

Alma nodded. She could do that. She would be happy to do that. She would be happy.

"Then come on inside. Get out of that cold," The nurse said and welcomed her in.

FORTY-FIVE

It was more than a storm. It was like being inside a sheet of ice. The wind and snow attacked his skin, tearing at him. Kinney staggered away from the figure in the snow, the mound of white and red. He sniffed the air, as if he could smell her, and moved . . . forward. The blood ran from his temple and dribbled down his cheek. He tasted the iron on his lips. His only thought now was to trudge forward. He was too cold to feel his body. He seemed to be propelled by some inner force. The Will Of God, perhaps. He knew the asylum lay within reach. Behind the gusts of wind, he saw the outline of her in the distance. That's where he would head.

Forward. One step at a time.

He spared no thoughts of Kostic's body in the snow. By morning, it would be fully covered. If anyone asked, he could tell them he was attacked. A poor psychiatric doctor attacked by a wayward inmate.

Kinney thought of reaching his wife and taking her back to his house and his bed and locking the doors. He was done with work and with trying to help mankind. He had plenty of money on which to live. He needed only his wife and the warmth of her body to help him feel alive. He needed nothing else.

He walked through the storm.

Just before he entered Building 50, he thought of a reason for the cut on his forehead and his condition. As an afterthought, he tossed the scalpel, the tip frozen with red and bits of brain matter, into the bushes. Maybe they'd find it in spring when the snow melted. Kinney doubted it. Many things were lost, never to be found again.

FORTY-SIX

Nurse Kolenda led Alma in through the front door. Alma shivered in the warmth of the building. She was home and not home. She wondered if maybe having been gone for so long, she might never feel like the place was home again.

"Can you start at once?" Nurse Kolenda asked.

Alma nodded. What else could she do? She was in a sort of shock, knowing her papa and her husband fought in the snow and the cold. She longed to return to the shadows of her former life, but also felt as if her duty lie with helping the people who had for so many years protected her existence.

"This way," the nurse said and walked briskly through the building. "We'll take the Tunnels to the women's ward," she said. "You'll need a uniform then you will help immediately with whatever needs doing." The nurse paused and turned to face her. "It's tuberculosis, dear. An epidemic. There is much death here I'm afraid."

"It's okay," Alma said softly. Death didn't scare her, the living did. "Let me lead. I know a faster way." Alma took her place in front of the nurse and walked to the tunnels, returning to the place of her own beginning.

FORTY-SEVEN

Outside, the wind swirled. Kinney's hands were ice. His face was ice. A deep, almost growl-like sound resonated in his chest. He coughed and spit bright red into the snow. He looked at his hands: red also. His shirt was red. His shoes–red. When you took a life by force, the body seemed to protest with violence. He was covered in the violence of Kostic's passing. He'd ripped the soul from Kostic's body, and it showed.

Kinney dipped his hands into the snow and scrubbed his hands. He could not get the red out.

The doors swung open to Building 50. He sniffed the air. He would have Rose soon. He could feel it.

"Doctor Kinney? Is that you?" He thought the behemoth Briggard called his name, but he couldn't be sure.

Kinney had sunk to his knees in the snow, and the growling in his chest became a roar, as if a beast crouched to leap free. He wanted to tell Briggard to bring him inside so he could take Rose home with him. He'd pulled Rose from the dead, brought her back in Alma's form, and he wanted her with him. He tried to explain but could no longer contain the beast within him.

"Oh, dear God," Briggard said. "You're sick, doctor."

Kinney didn't hear him. He coughed too hard, great spasms so raw and deep that a red rose spewed from his mouth and decorated the snow and froze there almost in the amount of time it took for Kinney to pass out into the coldness of night.

FORTY-EIGHT

Elliott Kinney was in the Nowhere.

Snow flew and shadows surrounded him.

He floated in ether. Heard the crashing of waves.
Looked down at his hands and saw them pushing down
Rose, holding her under the water until the sickness was out
of her body, taking her soul with it. He saw himself holding
Kostic under the water for treatment and countless others.
Saw their thrashing bodies under water as they resisted the
hydrotherapy. Why did so many patients resist him? Did
they want to keep their sickness close to them? Why not
surrender and give in to healing? Dr. Kinney was a healer.
He had a mission. And he would rescue souls by force, the
way he had finally freed his own wife, though her very life
force had flown from her body. In the last few moments,

when she looked peacefully up at him, he knew he had won, and the illness was gone. Liberated. He had liberated her.

He tried to move, but he could not. His chest burned. He coughed and seemed to cover himself with blood. How much blood? Why was this happening? Where was he? He could not think. He could not focus. He closed his eyes.

His mind flipped through pages and pages of new research. Doctors experimenting with new wonderful methods to take out a part of a person's brain, to find the actual source of their malignant spirit and pull it from them, wrench it free, leaving a person utterly peaceful. He'd heard of transformations, of wildly violent individuals suddenly as docile as lambs. How he longed to offer this healing, but for some reason, he could not steady the trembling of his hands.

He opened his eyes. It was dark now. He heard the peculiar music of a chorus of coughing. He knew, at once, where he was. He was a doctor here and now forced to be a patient.

"Let me up! Let me up!" he cried. "I have work to do!"

Feathers against his skin. A tickling of feathers. No, not feathers, but fingertips . . . and the scent of . . . what was that?

"What is that?" he whispered, his voice raw. "What is that smell?" Then he knew. He smelled flowers. He smelled . . . roses! Suddenly, a garden or roses surrounded him, and there . . . in the distant, his wife Rose called him. No. Not his wife. His sister! The real Rose! Calling to him.

177

Come to me, Elly, she called. *I want you with me.* She danced
and twirled, and he reached out to her. But when she spun to
face him it was not his Rose, it was the other woman, the one
who looked so much like his sister, but was only a cheap
imposter. Somehow, he had failed in making her become
Rose. Somehow, she remained . . . "Alma," he breathed.

"I am here," she whispered. Kinney knew the feathers
against his skin were the touch of her fingertips dancing over
him. But there were far too many fingertips, weren't there?

"Who else is here?" he said, his voice still strangled.

"Open your eyes, husband. Open them," Alma said
softly, her voice like wind and bells.

The shadows pulled back. The fog receded. And
Kinney saw . . . no . . . it wasn't possible! Patients of his—
patients long gone and buried. Kostic smiled at him, and the
old woman who was a sexual predator laughed at him, her
skirts lifted above her head to expose a patch of gray, twisted
hair between her legs. There was Elena who he had bent to
his will when he was first in medical school. She stared at him
with sightless eyes and pointed a broken finger at him as if in
accusation. There were nameless patients, ones who did not
survive his treatments or later died of heart attacks or drug
overdose. And there was a young boy with a rope around his
neck who ended his own life instead of endure any more of
Kinney's treatments. And there . . . there . . . was Rose. She
was there! And yet she looked angry.

"Stop touching me!" Kinney cried, but the fingertips
would not stop. They reached for him, his ghosts, his dead;

they touched him. Covered his body with their probing fingers, rough, smooth, young, and old. *Take him,* someone whispered. *Take him take him take him,* they echoed, a hundred voices joining in chorus.

"No!" He cried, his voice firm and strong now. "I have work to do!"

"I'm afraid your work here is done." It wasn't Alma who spoke this to him but Rose. The last thing Kinney saw was her smiling face then the pillow Kostic placed over Kinney's face.

And then . . .

Darkness.

Complete and utter.

Though he was still awake.

FORTY-NINE

Kinney's bed lay on the front porch of Building 50, surrounded by rows and rows of other patients in white beds, their pillows dotted with red.

"Do not watch him, dear. It does not do your spirit good," Mama Liliana said to Alma.

They stood in the shadows, where they were both so at home. Liliana wore nothing but a thin nightgown, the outline of her voluptuous body just visible beneath the gossamer threads. She looked as if she belonged in the asylum, as if she were a part of the place. Madness had seeped into the lines of her face, the spin of her long hair, but it had not etched itself with pain, but with acceptance. With an embrace. Sometimes a house or a church or an institution could reach its tendrils into the very fabric of a person and bind to them. This had happened to Liliana. She was a part of the hospital now, and she did not fight this. No. There was no need to fight that which you loved.

Alma, on the other hand, had changed. There was a time when she belonged in the shadows. When her very existence was a mad secret whispered through the tunnels that crisscrossed underground. Now, however, she stood clothed in her buttoned white dress, stretched taut over the new curve of her growing belly. The nurse's hat was pinned securely to her thick hair . . . and she looked at Kinney with the detachment that authority breeds. Alma was no longer an inmate in her house, but an authority.

"He's gone, you know. There's no hope for him. The sickness has him," Alma said. "But then, the sickness has always had him, hasn't it."

Liliana patted her on the back.

"I can get you out of here," Alma continued. "I have money now. I know people. I can set us up a house. For all of us. For you and Papa Beeler and . . . " She paused, knowing that her other parents, Papa Kostic and Mamma Grant, were gone now to that place of white from which they could never come back. Liliana did not answer this time. In fact, she had already disappeared into the shadows, so quickly and silently Alma wondered if she had ever been there at all.

The hospital shivered with the coughing of the dying.

Kinney tossed in his bed. Writhed. He was like a snake trapped in cloth and tried to free himself by endlessly turning, thus snaring him even more securely. His cough became a great crescendo. He clawed at his throat. He fought against his own body.

Alma could have gone to him and said, "This, this is what it feels like to be trapped. This is what you have done to so many of the ones that I have loved." Or perhaps, "Look! Look around you doctor! You are just like us, now!" Or maybe even, "You are not my husband, and I am not your wife, and you are not well. You are not sound."

He needed no curses from her. Justice was being delivered by an invisible hand. It reached into his mouth, swirled into his mind and took what was there, stole his breath and his heart . . . and it was this he choked on. Alma knew Kinney would have no tunnel of white light to pass through. His end would come with the coldness of not a caring soul.

It only took a minute or so, and it was over. Elliott Kinney gave up fighting. His body contracted, then released.

The ward fell silent for a moment as if relieved from his passing. Alma stared at him. He did not move. The child in her belly reached forward. Alma felt her child's caress inside her, as if to say goodbye.

Alma turned and walked down the hall.

Her footsteps faded into the darkness.

FIFTY

Three hundred and seventeen souls took flight during the tuberculosis epidemic, taking many of us along with it. Alma and the rest of the team of nurses and volunteers tended to them, cleaned their beds, soothed their coughs, and prepared their bodies for burial. She worked endlessly, at all hours of the day, and took over for Nurse Kolenda after she developed the telltale rattle in her chest. Nurse Kolenda recovered; many others did not.

When the epidemic passed and the halls emptied and were washed and polished again, the hospital returned to its former state as an asylum. Patients were locked in their wards. Treatments for their mental ailments resumed. A new doctor arrived on campus. He brought with him knowledge of a technique that would cure the most violent of patients of the terrible spirit writhing within them. By drilling holes into a skull, the mean spirits were released and the patient returned to life quieter, simpler, and (Alma thought) without any personality left. Later, the surgery would be replaced with the simple use of an icepick through the eye and into the frontal lobes of the brain. This, though, would be a decade in the future.

Alma grew big with child, and though everyone at the asylum knew she was pregnant, knew in fact that Doctor Kinney had placed it within her womb, the nurses and doctors responded with silence. They did not acknowledge the pregnancy; it was as if it didn't exist.

Mallie Lyn Peters returned to work at the asylum where she would take up duties as one of the cooks in the three cafeterias. She placed the food order with Charlie who brought her baskets of meat, cheese, fruits and vegetables. One day, he brought her a ring. We were happy for her. She had shown us kindness.

The moment he slipped the ring on her finger, far away, in the belly of the hospitals, Alma bit her lower lip and began to push.

Her daughter entered the world much as she did . . . in the shadows . . . but this time, hands welcomed her. A group of us had followed their favorite nurse down into the tunnels. We had not turned their backs to her pregnancy. In fact, we awaited it with anticipation, and Alma's daughter was greeted with laughter and joy.

Alma gave her new child her nipple to suckle. The baby girl pulled on it, and her lips smacked. The pain that ran through Alma's breast struck her as proof that her child was alive, and fierce with longing. She would grow strong and healthy, but, Alma told us, she would not grow up here.

On their wedding day, when Charlie carried Mallie Lyn over the threshold and into the small dusty space of their kitchen, a basket greeted them with a small child wrapped in hospital cloth. Mallie immediately heated some milk and soothed the screaming babe with milk dribbled from a cloth. The newlyweds did not discuss it. They looked at each other and simply nodded. They would call her Elizabeth. She was their daughter, for what does it matter where a person comes from or how they're brought into the world as long as once they are in it and swaddled in love?

Alma's daughter, and in a way our daughter, would not be hidden in the shadows of the Tunnels. She would move fiercely into the light, and she would be happy. We would see to that.

The End

STORIES

The Perfect Neighbor

I bought the house on Whippoorwill Dive all on my own. I fought for it; I worked for it; I prayed about it, and I'm not even a religious person. I don't know. I wanted to prove something to my ex and to myself. Maybe that I was actually capable of doing something on my own. The house was small but cozy. A perfect house for one. I didn't think of it as a Forever House, just an in-between house. A house in which to heal my heart and spirit.

After movers brought in what few boxes I had, I unpacked on my own and felt the weight of loneliness like a brick inside my stomach. So when my next-door neighbor stopped by with a batch of brownies still warm from the oven, I was touched. It seemed like the sort of thing housewives did in the fifties. It was quaint and cute. She even wore an apron!

"I see you're making quite a nest for yourself here," she said, nodding to my house. I had spent all morning painting my bedroom, changing it from an ugly bright yellow to a comforting deep brown. I wore paint-spattered clothes and my frizzy hair puffed out at the corners of an old baseball cap.

"I'm making it more of . . . oh, I don't know. More *me*."

She nodded and I could tell she understood. "Well, I just wanted to welcome you to the neighborhood. I've made you these brownies. They're shamefully gourmet. I'm a bit of an overachiever that way."

She handed me the brownies, and I could feel their warmth. In my mind I was already topping one with ice cream. "They smell perfect," I said.

"They are," she said with a slight smile and we both laughed. "I like things to be a certain way. What do they call it? OCD? But they don't call Martha Stewart that."

"Are you a Martha Stewart?" I thought she might be. Her lawn was a deep green next to my slightly browned one. She had planters that were hand painted in deep swirls of green and yellow and flowers that looked so perfectly in bloom that they could've been fake.

"Me? A Martha Stewart? No!" she laughed again and I think it was then that I realized something was a little off, but I ignored it. "I'm a Marilyn," she said as if that explained everything.

***

Marilyn and I became . . . friends. Yes. I guess that's the word for it. When I worked outside on the lawn, mowing or raking as the months passed, she would come out with freshly squeezed lemonade on a platter with a side of homemade cookies. In the summer the cookies were lightly scented with lavender from her garden; in the autumn she made apple cookies with apples from a tree in her backyard. She always wore a dress and looked attractive. Her hair was long and brushed until it shined. Her makeup could've been applied by a beautician. Her nails were manicured: perfectly shaped, the perfect shade of red.

As time passed and I sweated and struggled outside to maintain the lawn, it occurred to me that I never saw Marilyn leave her house. Nor did I ever see anyone enter it. Did she work? Did she date? Was she alone? If she was alone then why didn't she have the same frazzled look that I seemed to be stuck with? I could barely manage to pull myself out of bed and get ready to go to the office. And when I did, I somehow seemed to look ruffled . . . or at least like I needed an antidepressant.

Marilyn was so perfect she seemed to glow.

Autumn rolled around and the large tree in my front yard was such a deep orange, it seemed to have burst into flames. Eventually my tree shed the last of its leaves, except one still clung to a low branch, and for some reason it was green.

As I bagged the leaves (while in yoga pants, a stained t-shirt and my hair in a haphazard pony tail) I sensed rather than heard Marilyn approach.

"No, no, no!" she cried and then flung herself up towards that lone green leaf. Perhaps it was just my imagination of a play of the light, but for a moment her brightly painted nails seemed to look like talons as she swiped at the leaf. She tore it from the tree and crumpled it in her hand. I noticed that a strand of her perfect hair fell over one eye, hiding it. She carefully smoothed it back into place, took a deep breath and said, "That leaf was just out of place. It looks so much better now." She wiped her forehead with her hand and there was a thin line of dirt.

Certainly it was dirt and not, as my mind had tricked me into thinking, blood.

***

On Halloween night, Marilyn's house transformed into a cover of a magazine. She somehow had decorated the house overnight because when I awoke that morning, there were perfectly carved pumpkins lining the steps. A witch's pot boiling with dry ice. Piped in scary music echoing from the porch. There were spider webs that glistened and looked so real that the spiders crouching within them appeared as if they were about to give birth to a thousand babies. It made my skin itch. It was perfect.

I worked all day and didn't have the time or energy to carve pumpkins. I turned on my porch light, put out an un-carved pumpkin, and waited for the kids to come. I

191

envisioned handing out chocolates and being the Cool House. I'd actually purchased about twenty full-sized candy bars. One of the reasons my ex and I had divorced was that after ten years together, I decided I wanted children. He decided he wanted to buy a boat. I thought the children in their costumes would cheer me somehow.

I waited.

And waited.

But no children came. At least not to my house, and not to any of the other houses on the street—except Marilyn's. A steady stream of families drove up. Lovely, thin, perfectly coiffed women walked their children up to the door. They kissed their cheeks, and left quickly. It seemed strange to me that the children were older, probably twelve or thirteen, without costumes, and without siblings or friends. Each mother dropped off one child. The moms were so beautiful yet seemed sad. Perhaps, I thought, Marilyn was hosting a party for busy working moms. What a strange Halloween party it must be. There seemed to be no joy from any of the children.

At nine o'clock, when the steady stream of cars to Marilyn's had stopped and the street slipped completely into night, she came to my door. She was dressed as a witch, wearing full makeup. Her face was gnarled and twisted, her back humped, and her hands looked arthritic—no doubt bent from so many potions. She'd even disguised her voice. "Come to my house," she offered. "We'll have a pot of tea. I want to show you my Halloween collection."

Because I was lonely, because I waited so long, because Marilyn was so perfect at everything, because I was so inadequate, I did the only thing I could think of. I went to her house.

***

The inside of her house was as beautiful as the outside. In fact, it was like stepping into the pages of a magazine. Her lush living room featured a leather sofa, a perfectly roaring fireplace, and silk pillows in shades of crimson and burgundy.

She walked me through the kitchen with gleaming countertops and a silver fridge. There was an island made of some kind of expensive looking wood with a set of knives spread out as if she was ready to carve a Thanksgiving turkey.

"Did you have a nice party?" I asked her.

"Party?" her voice crackled. I wished she'd drop the old hag act. I was beginning to get annoyed by her Halloween get-up, and for a moment I dreaded Christmas. Would she don a Mrs. Claus outfit? Would there be elves?

"You know," I said, "all the kids?"

She cackled then. Yes. *A real cackle.* Her laughter sent shivers up my spine and somehow I knew. It was as if there was a spell of perfection over her house that shimmered and popped, the way a bubble shimmers and pops as soon as you've launched it into the air. I saw the perfection of her kitchen, and then I saw the kitchen as it really was. The dozens of Mason jars stacked on shelves. The piles of children's clothes in the corner. The blood smeared cutting board. The shadows. Oh, god . . . the shadows, everywhere.

I looked at Marilyn. I stared at her—and I saw. She wasn't wearing makeup. The slight green of her skin was its natural hue. Her pointed nose was her actual nose. And her fingers were, indeed, sharpened into talons.

"You see me now, don't you dear?" she asked. I broke out into a sweat. I couldn't speak, so I nodded instead. "And do you know what I keep in those jars?" She pointed to a row of jars above the stove. I didn't need to look at them because I knew. I knew. She kept children in those jars. Bits and pieces of them. Everywhere. An entire collection replenished every Halloween.

She pushed me gently forward. Led me into a small room that looked like a fortune-teller's lair complete with swaths of fabric, sparkling light, and a crystal ball in the center of a round table. "Sit," she ordered and I did. "Payment first."

As if in a trance I held out my palm but there was no money there. She dragged her nail across the palm, and a thin line of blood appeared. She brought my palm to her lips and I felt the leathery tickle of her tongue.

"I know what you want. You want what all the women who come to this neighborhood want. And you can have it. You can have it all, for a price."

I couldn't breathe. My heart hammered. I wanted to cry out, to run, but I was frozen there. "Tell me what it is your heart desires," she hissed, drawing out the last syllable.

I could not stop myself. I spoke the words. "I want children," I said. "I want love. I want a nice house. I want to be beautiful. I want things to be easy." It was as if all of my secret wishes simply floated to the surface, like bubbles of air.

"Yessss," she said. "And you will have it all."

***

I would like to say that I called the police and turned her in. I would like to say that I ran screaming and shouting for help. But I didn't. We shared some pumpkin bars, and then a special cup of tea. It was thick like cocoa, but bitter and she told me to drink every drop. Payment, she said, would not be due for fourteen years.

Fourteen years seemed so very far away.

I noticed the changes almost overnight. I began to lose weight. My hair grew long and shiny. Things came easier at work. In fact, I started to excel at almost everything. And then I met the man of my dreams. Franklin and I wed almost three months after meeting, and I conceived almost immediately.

I have long since moved from the house on Whippoorwill. We live in a seven bedroom, three-bathroom home in East Grand Rapids, Michigan. We have, I must admit, a picture perfect life. And with four beautiful children now, it seems the price will be almost worth it.

There is a price for this perfection. Would I change anything? If I hadn't met Marilyn, if I hadn't agreed to her terms, would I have the beautiful and easy life I have now? No.

I have tried not to love my firstborn, but it has been difficult. She was such an easy baby and now, at thirteen, I can see the woman she could become if the contract weren't due. My husband and I have not explained to her the price of perfection. We do not speak of it. It is something we know and accept. It is the way things are.

Tomorrow is Halloween and I will travel once more back to Whippoorwill Drive where Marilyn is waiting. She only shows her true face on Halloween so that she can perform the incantations she needs to make the magic happen. I will drop my daughter off at her front porch, and my daughter will go inside willingly, and I will drive home to my perfect family, and we will say a word of thanks for all our blessings.

The Shedow

Katie Mills had a conscience; she just chose not to use it. Life was short and she would not end up like her mother: catering to a husband who cared nothing for her. She'd watched her mother be beaten down by the years and the insults. Had witnessed the fading of her beauty and the actual escape of her spirit. And when her mother died, something hardened within Katie and she knew that whatever path she chose in life, it would be one of pleasure.

So she had enjoyed.

Now she was thirty-eight and she had the life and body that other women envied. She'd made a sizeable fortune as an attorney. What she couldn't afford to buy for herself, she could usually encourage one of her string of lovers to purchase for her. She had jewels and fine clothes and a sporty little car. Her body was as lithe and pert as it was when she was in her twenties. She detoxed every now and again, but mostly she enjoyed food when she wanted it. And she enjoyed sex when she wanted it, too.

A decade ago, she'd considered marrying, but the thought made her throat close up and she felt like she couldn't breathe. So much was wanted of women who were married. So much was demanded. A married woman aged suddenly, and surrendered the youth of her body to the children she carried. Katie didn't want kids. They were too loud and sticky. No. She found joy in food and wine and late nights with men. For the last ten years she'd followed a strict exercise regimen to keep her body thin and she had only one rule when it came to dating: she would only date married men. They were less complicated. Easily manipulated. And once you were finished with them, it was easy to send them on their way.

Just this morning, she had sent her most recent lover, Ted, home. He'd started to have that glassy in-love look to his eyes and had started referencing a future that included 'we'. "I was thinking we could take a little holiday," he'd said. And then, "I think, Katie . . . I think I might be falling in love with you."

"Stop it," she'd said and laughed, though she meant the words. She moved her hands down the slope of his chest. He was five years younger than her and his body was still perfect. In another five years though, that skin would slacken and his belly would pouch and he would be of no use to her then. He was almost no use to her now. As soon as the word 'love' was mentioned, Katie knew it was just a matter of days. Maybe even hours.

To shut him up, she'd kissed him hard, hungrily, and then kept him busy before sending him to the gym to shower before going home to his po-dunk wife. The Wife, Emma or something, was like many of the wives: a stomach that perpetually looked like she was five months pregnant; hair that was frizzing and needing a dye job; legs that she hadn't shaved in months. She probably smelled of milk, from tending to their kids.

What an awful hell to be trapped in, Katie thought, and before she could feel too much sympathy for the woman, she dismissed her. Ted had been fun. More fun than most of them. He'd known intuitively how to fuck her, and when he needed instruction, he listened and did what she told him. In many ways he was perfect, if he could just have kept his heart out of it.

Katie pulled the sheets from the bed. She could wash them, but it seemed like a lot of effort. Instead, she wadded them up and stuffed them in the trash. Tonight, she would tell him she was sick. Instead, she would get dressed up, meet her girlfriends at the bar and meet someone new.

There was always someone new. Always some lonely soul who needed just a little flirtation and he was yours. Men were pliable and so easy to convince to forget their vows.

She laughed to herself, pulled on her yoga pants and shirt, and decided to head out to the gym for a meditation class. When she heard the slight knocking at her door, she assumed it must be one of the annoying neighborhood kids trying to sell overpriced chocolate.

"If you really want a dollar, just ask for one," she said as she opened the door . . . but standing in front of her was not a child proclaiming to raise funds for a non-existent basketball team, but a short, frazzled-looking woman with lines in her face and a stomach that bespoke of having given birth to more than one child.

The woman pointed at her, a pudgy finger shaking. "Katie Mills," she said. It wasn't a question.

And Katie understood who this was. This was Emma, Ted's wife. Or perhaps it was some other man's wife. Did it matter? Did she care? Every once in a while, a brave wife would seek her out. Their interaction never satisfied the women. They weren't really angry at her specifically, but what she represented. Their fury would be better served by divorcing their husbands, not yelling at her.

"What do you want?" Katie asked with a sigh. She wanted to do yoga and relax a little. She wanted to shower. She wanted to meet and fuck someone tonight who wasn't Ted and didn't talk about ridiculous things like love.

"I know who you are. I know what you do. Have you no morals? Have you no sense of decency?"

Katie almost laughed. The woman even had a slight accent. Slavic or something. Something foreign. She was pathetic. Katie could pretend she didn't know what the woman was talking about, but she was bored and tired and she had places she wanted to go. "You want to blame me for giving your husband one of the greatest night's of his life? Fine. Blame me. You should be thanking me. I entertain him and then he can go back to you and support you. And if you'd just take better care of yourself, maybe this wouldn't have happened in the first place. For crying out loud, lady, you look like a grandmother." Katie did laugh then: a sharp laugh, more of a bark really. "Now leave me alone."

The woman did not move. She cocked her head. Her frizzy hair lifted in a slight breeze. Then she raised her pudgy fingers again and pointed two of them at Katie's heart. "You want to be left alone? You will be left alone. And when you are all alone, that's when she will come."

Katie huffed. An angry, crazy, jealous wife. Could she be anymore cliché? "Who's going to come?" she asked, more to get the woman to shut up and get off her doorstep than anything.

"The Shedow," The woman said. It sounded like she-doe. Then after a breath, the woman repeated the words quickly in succession three times. "The Shedow. The Shedow. The Shedow." The woman dropped her hand, turned and hurried to her waiting car.

Katie shut the door and locked it. The Shedow? What kind of backwards threat was that? What the hell was a Shedow? Some kind of Slavic plague, or something? A guy who would threaten to break your legs? Indigestion?

She laughed to herself. Women were pathetic. They always blamed the lover and not the husband. Katie went to grab her car keys and noticed there was a thin, dark strip on

201

her wall. Funny how she'd never noticed that. It was almost as if the light didn't quite reach the corner. She turned on the lamp and the darkness disappeared.

At least that had been an interesting interaction. Certainly one she could tell her girlfriends about later. She could almost hear herself telling them, "You will never believe what happened to me today. Some fat gypsy woman threatened me with The Shedow."

As soon as she thought the words, the back of her neck prickled just as the light exploded. Katie jumped. There must have been some kind of power surge or something. Before leaving her house, she reminded herself to get some new light bulbs. Those annoying energy-efficient kind. That thin strip of shadow was back on the wall again and for some reason it made her slightly uncomfortable.

*

"I'm really sorry, Katie. I just can't get together today. Matt and I have Date Night. Maybe next week if I can get a sitter."

"Of course. No problem. I totally understand." She said her goodbye and pressed END on the phone. Strange. Her three regular girlfriends all had dates. One didn't even return her call. So Katie had started calling friends that she hadn't seen in ages. Many of them were married now with kids. One of them even said to her "Uh, no. I don't really want to see you ever again. Have you forgotten what you did with my boyfriend?" Katie had forgotten. That had been ages ago. Women were so petty.

Still. She'd picked up sushi at the grocery store and didn't actually need to go out for lunch. Lunch with her friends had gotten boring lately anyway. They wanted to talk about their relationships and where they were vacationing and what they needed to fix in their houses. Katie talked about whom she was dating now. Last time, her best friend Catherine had even dared to say: "I just don't know how you do it. All these married guys. You must be pretty lonely." Lonely? What a laugh! Katie had more fun than any of them put together. She lived the kind of life you saw in magazines. All she lacked was the paparazzi following her around.

It was Saturday night and she didn't need anyone to go out and have fun. She wasn't about to stay in and watch television. She'd go out on her own. She'd get dressed up and go out. Or, she thought, she could just call one of her past boyfriends. She'd call Ted. He was probably out on the street now anyway. His crazy wife had certainly kicked him out. And Ted loved her. Ted wanted to be with her. Ted wanted to vacation with her. He'd probably propose to her someday and maybe she'd even allow that.

She pressed his number on the phone now and it went quickly to voice mail. "Hi, baby. So listen . . . I had a visitor this morning and I just want to make sure you're okay and you can come over if you want. I'll leave the door open for you. I . . . " She cleared her throat. It was strange that it went so quickly to voice mail. He'd always picked up before, even when he was in a meeting, or at a restaurant with his wife and kids. "I think I might be falling in love with you too," she said quickly, trying the words out as if trying on a new coat. She didn't mean the words; it was just something to say to convince him to come over. She wanted him here. She wanted to kiss him. And she wanted him to look at the strange dark strip on the wall.

Katie went upstairs to get ready for the evening. She had no concrete plans, but either Ted would come over or she would go get a drink at the bar and meet someone.

Her room was dark. In the corner was a patch of darkness that was deep and long, as if a tree trunk were casting a shadow. She flicked on the light and the darkness evaporated.

She needed a drink and to get out of the house. She needed someone to talk to, just to take the chill out of the silence.

She turned on some music and began to undress. And then she heard a slight whispering sound, like the sound a too-long dress makes as it drags across the floor.

Katie turned up the music and began to sing.

***

The Shedow. The Shedow. The Shedow.

She woke up in her bed, her body warm and slick with sweat, and that woman's words repeating in her mind. Ridiculous. The Shedow. What was that anyway? You could scare anyone by simply whispering something repetitively. If someone said, in a whisper-crazy voice, *That cake is coming for you* . . . you would spend the rest of the day looking over your shoulder in the hopes you weren't being chased by a menacing baked good.

There was no such thing as a Shedow. Whatever *that* was. A she-doe? A super feminine deer? Some kind of Japanese liqueur?

Katie turned on all her lights. Already it was dark outside. She had no idea what time it was. Perhaps that yoga class really took it out of her. Or last night's sex.

She looked at the clock, wondering if she had time to get ready. She'd go clubbing tonight. She'd meet up with some of her acquaintances at the bar, pretend that she'd been stood up or something. There would be an awkward ten minutes or so of drinking alone and then she'd see someone she knew or she'd meet some horny guy with his wedding ring in his pocket. As if that fooled anyone.

It was awfully dark though. She reached for her phone and was startled at the display. 2:30. 2:30 AM. She'd slept most of the night away. There was no point going out now. Everyone was already drunk and hooking up, or past the hook up and passed out naked next to each other. She'd have to spend the night alone.

Alone, she thought, and laughed. She needed some time alone.

She scrolled through her phone and saw that she'd missed three voicemails from Ted. Her heart leapt a little. He wanted to come over. He was through with his crazy wife. Well, Katie would call him and let him come over and then she'd work on meeting someone new later. Tonight though, he would be a warm body next to her and maybe he'd make her room feel a little less dark. The shadows seemed to be creeping in on her.

She grabbed her robe and slipped it on. She'd listen to his messages downstairs on her couch. She'd turn on the TV and fill the house with sound. On her way, she turned on every light. It was such a dark night and for some reason she felt like she needed it to feel like day. Must be the lost hours.

Curled up on her couch, she pressed play on the first message. He would say he loved her. He would ask her where she was and was the door open. He would . . .

"Katie. Listen, I know . . ." there was a scratching sound that covered up some of his words. A bad connection. He was speaking fast. "Don't call me or text me. I made a horrible mistake, I love . . ." the scratching continued " . . . my wife. She's everything to me. I don't know what I was thinking. Just . . . don't. Call."

The message ended. He didn't even say goodbye.

It made no sense. He had said just last night that he loved her. Wanted to be with her. He was over his wife and . . . she pressed play on the second message. This time his voice was a hush.

"Something's coming for me. I know it. It moves in the dark. Shit. It can only move in the dark. I love my wife. Do you understand! I am sorry for what I did to her!" There was a pleading in his voice.

Katie was afraid to press the next message.

She pressed play.

At first she wasn't sure what she was hearing. Laughter? A scratching noise? What was that? It sounded like the swishing of skirts. And then the faintest . . . He was crying. Into the phone. "I'm so sorry," he said between sobs. "Please." And then "No, god, please. Turn on the light. She's going to get me! Please!"

And then he screamed.

A real scream. The scream of a man at the end. And there was a horrible sound, something slithering. Licking. Lapping. And after the scream came a hush of static. Or the sound of someone saying "Shhhh".

Katie tossed the phone away from her. Of all the messed-up, manipulative crap to pull. Clearly Ted was in on it with his wife. He was trying to freak her out. Trying to get into her brain.

Another idea occurred to her, an idea inspired by the scream on the phone. What if Ted wasn't in on it? What if his wife had threatened Katie, and then went home and . . . did something . . . to him? What if those sounds, those awful sounds of chewing, what if she'd killed him and recorded it so Katie would hear?

She reached for the phone again. She'd call the police. She'd play the messages for them. She clicked the button and swiped the screen but the phone would not turn on, as if its battery had just gone out.

There was a sudden power surge in the house and the lights flickered. The TV sparked and went out. For a terrifying moment Katie was in the dark. It took a moment for her eyes to adjust before she saw the woman step from the shadows. The lights flickered on. There was no one there.

She was seeing things. All was well. Her house was fine. Her imagination had taken over. And then, the light farthest from her popped and went out, and then Katie saw her. The Shedow. She moved in shadows, or generated shadows. There was a line of light in front of her and the swirling black smoke reached out to the light but not beyond. Then another light popped, extending the darkness, and the woman took another step forward.

In a series of pops and hisses, all the lights went out.

For a moment, Katie sat in darkness. She thought perhaps her eyes were closed, but then she saw the slightest movement in front of her. The woman stepped free from the whirlwind of shadow. She seemed to glide across the room, the black smoke around her legs as if it were a long dress. The woman looked at her, dress swirling, dark hair floating around her head as if she were underwater. Katie closed her eyes for a moment, but when she opened them, the woman was closer. She was almost to her.

This was the Shedow. Katie believed now. She knew now. The woman cocked her head, smiled, and then flicked her long tongue. She reached the impossibly white and slender finger out, out, and traced the line of Katie's pulsing neck with her black fingernail that was more like a talon.

Katie knew real fear then and regret. She felt true sorrow for the choices she had made and the people she had harmed. But of course, it was too late. The Shedow grasped her arm in her claws and drew it to her mouth to begin a slow and maddening feast.

#

Birth Day

Amelia sat at her kitchen table with her tablet reading the North Quadrant Times. It didn't matter which site or news service she clicked on, every headline was nearly identical, with the exception of a few small words: *Birth Day Is Nigh! Birth Day Dawns! Beware of Birth Day!*

Articles were the same, too. All women aged 14–40 should prepare for oncoming labor. Do not go to the nearest hospital. If every woman went into labor at the same time (and that was what was expected) then hospitals would be overwhelmed and would not be able to help. No. The Birthing could be done at home. They'd had nine months to prepare. Everyone else, from young children, to older adults, to all the men, should check their birthing kits, re-watch delivery webinars, and prepare for . . .

Well. The articles were vague on what (or who) exactly to prepare *for*. The nearest guess was to prepare for a child. A billion children, actually, all over the world in every location: villages in Africa, deserts in America, and in the tallest urban jungles in the world. Even two doctors stationed at the North Pole had conceived, and they were both women without any men for thousands of miles.

Doctors and mathematicians calculated that Conception Day occurred on 17 April at 2:11:00 GMT. They had been crunching numbers since then to decide if the Conception or Birth Day had any astrological meaning. Their decision so far was . . . maybe.

Amelia was not worried. She ran her hands over her swollen abdomen and the child shifted within her. Fluttered, really. As if it had wings. And couldn't it? Her child could have wings, right? Stranger things happened. Stranger things *did* happen nearly nine months ago when every woman on the planet within a specific age range had conceived. When the news started pouring in, when understanding started dawning, the news sites trumpeted the findings: *Massive Simultaneous Teenage Pregnancy* became *All Women Above 14 Are Pregnant!* Amelia held her breath, hoping against hope. And then the new headlines: *No Women Over 40!*

She had cried into her pillow that night. Amelia had felt that she was different. She hoped that finally, after all these years, that she could have a child of her own. It was not to be. All the incoming data, every news site, and every expert claimed to understand: All the women in the world

211

between the ages of fourteen and forty were pregnant. There were no pregnancies before or after that age. Women who had been pregnant at the time of Conception Day, seemed to have reverted their pregnancies back to Conception Days. As if their pregnancies had simply restarted. No one over the age of forty had conceived. They were safe. Except . . . against all the data . . . except Amelia.

Amelia. Pregnant. But that was impossible. She was 43. She'd had fertility treatments back when she was married. The doctors had said it was impossible for her to conceive and then, inconceivably, Patrick had left her and started a family with someone else. But now? Now, this? A gift? From her research, she discovered that she was the only 43-year-old in the entire world who was also part of this experience, and because of this, she had sequestered herself. No one must know. No one must know that she was the one person who didn't fit. She'd seen what scientists had done in the beginning to understand. Those women they'd tested, experimented on, tried to help with terminating the pregnancy, those women had never come home. Young girls terrified of what their parents might think had tried aborting their fetuses . . . and ended up dying. Or worse. She knew there was something worse than death. There were weeks and weeks of agony while the cells within them shifted to create another fetus to replace the one they'd taken, only growing double and triple time and causing deep pain. Those girls, they were lost. Their spirits slipped away. After Birth

Day, Amelia wondered if they would come back to the world, but she doubted it.

She felt for them, these girls and scared women who were too terrified of carrying a child. She pitied them their lack of faith. She understood what it was like to feel lost, because she had been lost too, but in a different way. How she had slipped through living day to day, with no love in her life, just work, and sex occasionally, and long nights spent on her own while Patrick . . . She did not finish the thought. She reminded herself that now, with her child almost with her, she would be found.

There was no astrological or spiritual rhyme or reason for the moment of conception; she knew that. It was simply a miracle. Simply a miracle. Yes. She believed that this miracle was simple. A fact. Perhaps it was a leap of evolution. Whatever it was, there was no changing it, no stopping it, and the entire world had been forced to accept it. Birth Day was coming. Birth Day was nigh.

Amelia knew—at her very core—that there was, however, a reason why of all the women on the world she was chosen to be the oldest. Her child would be special. Her child would be a leader of children. She was chosen because her wanting had been so great; her suffering for a child so prolonged. Birth Day would change the world, beginning with her own.

"Incoming call," said the computerized (though entirely natural sounding) Voice. "It's your sister."

Amelia quickly stood and went to her kitchen counter. She smoothed her long red hair and pinched her cheeks, hoping to bring them some color. Though, actually, since becoming pregnant, she did seem to have an otherworldly glow. One of the many reasons she tried to stay inside. The hologram would dull her glow, but it could not dull the size of her stomach. If she stood behind the counter then her sister would not see her rounded belly on the vidscreen. Amelia only needed to keep her secret a bit longer. Birth Day was only hours away. And then she could tell the world of her purpose.

"Amelia!" Her sister said. Her voice was high and tight, her face pale. Her image stood across from Amelia, so clear that it was almost as if they could share a cup of coffee together. She seemed to have aged another ten years in just these nine short months. Her red hair was now streaked with white, and the color seemed to have tarnished. She had deep circles under her eyes and her skin was dry and creased with new wrinkles. "Why aren't you over here? You're supposed to bring your Birthing Kit! The orders say that family members must help other family members! It says! You agreed! We need you here!"

"I can't come. I'm sorry," Amelia said softly. She *was* sorry too. Sorry that her sister would have to deliver her grandchild on her own. Sorry for her niece who, at just shy of fifteen, was terrified of what was happening to her body.

Her sister began to cry. She tried to muffle her voice. "Please," she pleaded, looking straight into Amelia's eyes.

"Amelia . . . you're the only one who has any medical training. Ed is a complete moron. He's out back preparing the old bomb shelter in case some kind of attack happens. The boys are no help. I can't do this alone. Margie is only fourteen! She's just a child!" The rest of her words were lost.

Amelia took a deep breath. "It's going to be okay, Neener," she said using her sister's pet name. When Amelia was a baby, she called her sister Neener because she could not say *Nina*. "I'm telling you that the Birth Day is going to go fine. Margie can do this. You can do this. All you need . . . " Amelia took a sharp breath as a contraction gripped her. "All you need to do is believe."

Nina rubbed her eyes with the back of her hand, dragging a line of mascara across her face. "Believe what," she said and her words were filled with utter loss. "There's nothing left to believe in anymore. We don't even have control over our own bodies."

"Believe in miracles," Amelia said. "I do." She decided then that the time had come. She stepped away from the counter and walked to her sister's image standing before her.

"Amelia . . . " her sister breathed, as if she couldn't believe what she was seeing. She reached out to touch Amelia's stomach and then the connection was cut.

Amelia bent over as another contraction rippled through her body. The pain reminded her of surfing. How you rode the wave as long as you could until you tumbled, then, waiting in the water, you floated, until you could catch the next wave bringing you closer to shore. She would ride this out.

"Warning," called the Voice. "Birth Day is imminent. Prepare your delivery stations. Please tune into Quadrant Four's webcast delivery. Doctors are standing by to assist virtually. Remember: hospitals are not equipped to handle Birth Day. You must do this at home. Hospitals are on stand-by for emergencies, should any arise."

It seemed that even the computerized Voice was strained with fear and anticipation. This is what they had all been waiting for. The final answer was coming! What would happen next? Every time they'd tried to do a 3D imaging sequence, machines shut down. When a pregnant woman was in an accident and killed, they had tried to open her stomach to see what lurked within, but by the time they did that, the fetus had been absorbed. They'd tried ultrasounds and video feeds and even shamans to tell the world what kind of children women were growing. Would they be regular children? Gods? Demons?

Amelia knew the answer. She was growing Hope. Hope in the way that old advertisements claimed *Hope For a New World and a Better Tomorrow!*

The next contraction was fierce and Amelia leaned against a chair for support. She only needed to get to the next room where she had everything waiting. It was only a few more steps.

"Warning!" the Voice called. "The Children are coming!"

Amelia walked the few steps to her living room and lay down on the bed. She knew what was coming and that she only had to surrender to the experience and she would be okay. She breathed.

"Birth Day has begun!"

It happened incredibly fast. There was pain and tearing and she breathed through it. She was silent, in fact. All was silent. She no longer heard the Voice proclaiming warnings and advice for complications. She no longer heard the proclamations of the names of women who had successfully brought a child into the world, though she knew that there would be proclamations. She was aware that the world was in an orgiastic state of fear and anticipation. She knew that today people would take their own lives rather than learn of what was coming. She knew that what was coming was not, in fact, evil, but humanity's next leap into a bold new future.

She breathed. She pushed. And then the child slipped from her in a rush. There was silence. Amelia pushed herself up, scooped the child up, and looked into her daughter's perfect silver eyes. Her eyes seemed to spark with electricity. In fact, staring into the child's eyes, Amelia thought for a moment she saw the swirl of a tiny universe forming. The child seemed to consider her for a moment. Amelia brought her daughter's gleaming metallic body to her breast, kissed the top of her cool head, and smiled as her baby nursed, seeming to know exactly what to do.

Everything would be different now. This was how transformation happened: quickly, without warning, and if you were brave enough to embrace it, it would take you to incredible places. Amelia and her daughter, Hope, would lead them all.

"Warning" called the Voice. "The children! The children have arrived!"

All over the world people waited to hear the crying of the new children and were astounded when instead of sobs of a billion newborns, they heard the tinkling laughter of what they could only understand as stars.

Acknowledgments

"Tunnel Vision" was a direct result from a challenge I presented to readers on my blog. I gave several options on what I should write next and after posts and voting, they picked a historical gothic story.

I was raised in Traverse City, Michigan and my mom (Anne Knaggs) worked in Mental Health. She did crafts for a place called The Friendship Center, a day center for adults with mental and sometimes physical disorders. Growing up, I spent a lot of time at my mom's work, since she was a single mom. I even went to a summer camp and competed with the adults in sack races and the talent show. At the age of eleven, I didn't know the words for their disorders (words like schizophrenic, OCD, bipolar, etc.) I just knew that the people were different and everyone had their own little quirks. I knew whom to avoid and whom I could talk to.

Years later, my mom worked at a new day center that was housed in the State Hospital, a beautiful sprawling campus that was originally called "The Northern Michigan Insane Asylum". When I was eighteen, she took me on a tour of some of the facility, including the tunnels underneath. I only got to see a little bit of it, but it was enough to haunt me until, well, now.

So that's how "Tunnel Vision" came about. First, because of my blog, and then from little pieces of my upbringing that I've always been fascinated by. I'm also intrigued by the question of insanity and its definition. Dr. Kinney in this piece is the villain, of course, but I don't think doctors are villains. In fact, I think they do great work. But I needed a character that would be in the position to control and manipulate on a primal level, so that's where he comes from.

I have lots of people I'd like to thank for encouraging me to write this piece. It's by no means a perfect novella, but I am proud of it. So, in alphabetical order, here are people who helped push me to get this puppy written:

Janel Atwood Heird

Tim Beeler

Melissa Baldwin White

James B. Bradshaw

Patrick L. Callahan

Alexa Dannenberg

Tristan De Boer

Bettie Ellens

Christopher Grooms

Sydney Groth

Ginny Hebert

Evan Heird

Alysia Hough

T.M. Hunter

Diana Peffer Johnson

Anne Knaggs

Kit Kolenda

Bob Kostic

Kim McNiel Smith

Malinda Peterson

Roxanne Riley Victor

Deborah Rosko

John Shull

Liliana Juracán Stephenson

Kerri VanderHoff

Katie Wibert

Cory Young

A special thanks to Cheryl Sterling for her editing of "Tunnel Vision" and an even more special thanks to David Kolenda, who just happens to be my husband AND he edited "Tunnel Vision", the short stories, designed & formatted the book, turned it into something tangible, and put up with all my angst while writing this.

About The Author

Tanya Eby is a novelist and narrator and lives in Michigan with her tiki-obsessed husband and two quirky kiddos. Find out more about her work and her life by visiting her blog: tanyaeby.com. You can also find her on Twitter @Blunder_Woman and on Facebook at facebook.com/TanyaEbyWriter.